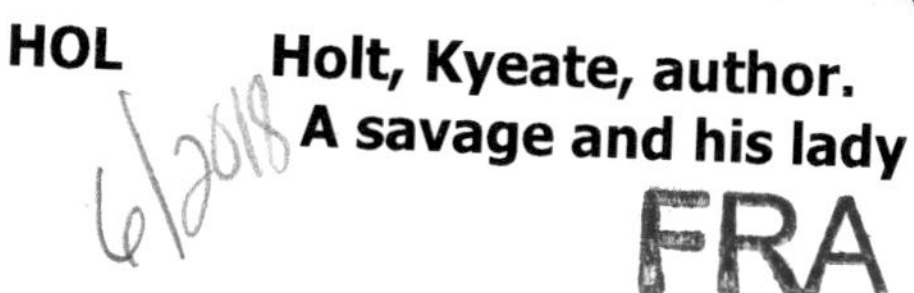

A Savage and His Lady

Dinero and Kyra's Story

By Kyeate Holt

A Savage and His Lady

Published by Mz. Lady P Presents

www.mzladypresents.com

Acknowledgements

First off, I would like to thank everyone who has been on this journey with me. I have been pushing so hard with lots of sleepless nights and headaches.

I thank my children who have been a tremendous push by asking me day in and day out "What's your word count?" and celebrating each time I hit a milestone.

I want to thank my publisher Mz. Lady P, for giving me the chance of a lifetime. I never thought I would be a writer for someone who books I am a fan of.

"You can want success all you want, but to get it, you can't falter. You can't slip, you can't sleep. One eye open, for real and forever." Jay-Z

Connect with me

Facebook: Author Kyeate Holt

Facebook Group: Kyeate's Book Club

Instagram: @adjustnmykrown

Twitter: @AdjustnMyKrown

Chapter 1

Lying across my bed, I was looking at pictures in my old photo album. A smile crept across my face when I came across a picture of Dinero and me on our first day of school in Kindergarten. My mom took this picture while we were at the bus stop. I flipped the page and laughed at another picture of the both of us on Halloween when I was ten. Dinero was a great part of my life. We did everything together. When I say everything, I meant just that. Dinero was my protector, not that anyone bothered me, but he gave me a feeling of being safe. Even when were little, he looked out for me.

Over the years, I can tell our feelings for each other had reached a different level. We lost our virginity to each other and all. You would think well why aren't y'all together? You and everyone around us think the same thing. We felt we would just experiment with each other rather than with people we weren't comfortable with. Things took a turn when I went to college. I was a freshman at Tennessee State University, and I remember it like it was yesterday.

Walking across the campus, I was heading to my second class of the day. I had my headphones in and was vibing to the music, something to make my walk a little bit quicker. I noticed a group of guy's standing in the yard, but I quickly diverted my attention elsewhere when I made eye contact with one guy. I saw him smile and head my way. I tried to pick up the pace, and I felt someone grab my arms. I turned around, and he was smiling at me. I saw his lips moving, but I couldn't hear him. This guy made me nervous, and I wasn't thinking straight. He reached up and removed my earbuds from my ear.

"That's better. How you doing, Ms. Lady?" he asked.

I looked him over, and he was every bit of fine. He was huge he looked to be about six feet tall. His beard was huge, and he rocked a curly man bun on top of his head. His shirt wasn't tight, but it fit him perfectly. I could tell he had tattoos everywhere.

"I'm fine," I said.

"You sure are. I can see you go here; where are you headed?" he asked.

"I was on my way to class; I've never seen you around. Do you attend here?" I asked.

"Nah baby, I just be here handling business. You should let me take you out sometime?" He lifted his brow as if that was an actual question.

"I guess that will be okay," I said. He reached into his pocket and pulled out his phone handing it to me. I put my number in his phone and handed it back to him.

"My name is Nitro," he said, looking at his phone "I'm gone hit you up later, Kyra. You get to class," he said. I smiled and hurried off to class.

After class that day, Dinero had come by and picked me up like he always did. Dinero didn't go to college; he said it wasn't for him. He worked at Wendy's. At times, I swear it was like he didn't want better for himself. He did save up and get him a tote your note car. It wasn't everything, but it got us from point A to point B. When Dinero picked me up, I got in the car and greeted him with a peck on the cheek.

"How was your day, lil' ugly?" he asked.

"It was cool. I met this guy today," I said, looking over at Dinero to see how he would react. He nodded his head

"That's what's up," he said.

I could tell he was mad. That's the shit we did; we would never act on being with each other, but as soon as someone enters the picture, it was a problem. My phone beeped, I looked down, and it was a text from Nitro. I chuckled.

"What's this nigga's name?" Dinero asked me.

"Nitro," I said, continuing to look at my phone. Dinero looked at me

"Nitro? Really, Ky. Of all niggas, you pick the grimiest nigga in the hood." Dinero said.

After that conversation, Dinero had been acting ill ass fuck whenever I mentioned Nitro. Nitro and I relationship took off fast. He wasn't rich, but I could tell he sold drugs to get his money. I wasn't used to being spoiled and getting whatever I wanted. Nitro kept my pockets laced, and Dinero just settled.

I closed the photo album and laid it on my dresser. I stood in front of my floor length mirror and looked at myself. I was easy on the eyes. My peanut butter complexion always had a glow to it. My skin stayed blemish free. I had a butt and breasts, thanks to my mama. Half of these chicks walked around looking fake as hell half the time. That wasn't my cup of tea.

"Kyra, Dinero is down here waiting on you? You act like this boy ain't got to go to work his damn self!" mama yelled, walking into my room. I continued to look in the mirror, making sure my hair was in place.

"I'm coming," I said.

I ran my hands through my natural curls and was satisfied with my look. Mama stood at the door shaking her head.

"You do all this prep work every time he comes around, yet you can't tell him how you feel about him," mama said, coming over to stand behind me in the mirror. I rolled my eyes

"Really ma, it doesn't even matter. I'm with Nitro." I looked in the mirror and heard ma suck her teeth.

"Nitro's ass ain't nothing but trouble. Who is here to pick you up and take you where you need to go whenever you call no questions asked? But go ahead don't listen to me because I don't know nothing right?" mama said, walking out of my bedroom.

Mama was right, but I wasn't about to tell her that. Dinero and I have been attached at the hip all our lives. As we got older, the feelings for him have of course intensified to that of a more romantic level. Little did mama know we had already been intimate plenty of times. I loved Dinero, but he didn't want shit out of life, plus I was already with Nitro.

Dinero never pushed the issue of us being together, so I never pushed it. I could tell he wasn't happy with me being with Nitro, but he never threw salt on the next nigga. Walking downstairs, I saw Dinero sitting on the couch having a deep conversation with mama, ain't no telling what they were talking about.

"I'm ready," I said, making my presence known.

Dinero looked up, and my panties instantly got wet. He stood up, put his hands in his pockets, and licked his lips. It was late September, so he wore a Nike Jogger suit and a pair of Foamposites. I was dressed down for a simple trip to Walmart but still could turn a head or two. I had on a pair of Seven7 Jeans with a white tee and a Victoria Secret PINK bomber jacket and some PINK slides, courtesy of Nitro.

"Bout time, you took all day just to come out wearing jeans and a t-shirt," Dinero said. I rolled my eyes.

"Shut up nigga, you never know who you gone run into at Wal-Mart," I said. "You need anything, ma?" I turned and asked my ma.

"Nah, I'm good," she said.

While in the car, I looked over at Dinero while he nodded to the music weaving his way through traffic.

"Why you keep staring at a nigga, Ky?" Dinero asked, turning the music down.

"Just thinking about mama's ass and why she's always pressuring us to be together," I said. Dinero grinned.

"That's because everyone knows we made for each other, but all you want a nigga for is this dick," Dinero said. I punched him in his arm.

"Nigga whatever, yo ass been hooked since you got a taste," I said. Dinero's phone went off. I grabbed it and looked at the phone "Ooh, who is Tori?" I teased but was slick jealous.

"Give me my phone, dude. Tori's just my friend," he said, grabbing his phone.

I bit my bottom lip and looked out the window as we arrived at Wal-Mart and parked. I grabbed the handle to get out the car

"You getting out?" I turned and looked at Dinero.

"Nah, go ahead I'm gone wait," he said. I shrugged my shoulders getting out the car and slamming the door.

Walking into Wal-Mart, my nerves were getting the best of me. Who the hell was this Tori chick, and why haven't I heard of her? We always tell each other about people we meet. That was the least of my worries though; I needed to be worried about my main reason for coming to Wal-Mart. I walked on the aisle looking at the many different boxes. I grabbed two and headed towards the register. After paying for my items, I headed back to the car and noticed Dinero on the phone. I got in the car and waited for him to end his call.

"Aite, I'll hit you up later," he said to who I assume whoever this Tori chick was.

"You get what you needed?" he asked. I nodded my head yes and continued to look out the window.

Dinero started up the car and pulled out. "*Your love is wonderful, yeah, and I don't wanna lose you. So, baby soon as I get home,*" Faith Evans boomed through the speakers, and I perked up. Looking at Dinero, we both started singing in unison along with Faith Evans the entire ride back to my place.

"Man, do you remember in middle school when my ass left for camp and I sang this to you?" I asked Dinero.

"How could I forget? You butchered that shit," Dinero said. I rolled my eyes.

"Chill out, mane. I'm just fucking with you. That will forever be our song. What you about to do?" he asked, looking at me. I got nervous not wanting to tell him the truth

"Nothing probably chill out. I'm meeting up with Nitro in the morning," I said. Dinero shifted in his seat.

"Oh well, I'm finna get up with Tori. I'll holla at you later," he said, brushing me off. It's funny how both our attitudes change when we mention other people.

"Aite," I said, getting out the car.

Walking into the house, my feelings were all over the place. My phone beeped, and I looked at my phone. It was Nitro.

"Hello," I spoke into the phone.

"Wassup boo?" Nitro's voice came through the phone.

"Nothing, I just walked in the house," I said.

"Word, where you been?" he asked.

"Dinero ran me to Wal-Mart," I said, entering my room and placing my things on the bed.

"Why you ain't call me? You always call that nigga to do shit for you that I'm supposed to do," he said.

"What does it matter, he just ran me around the corner. Wassup tho?" I asked really hoping to get off the phone.

"You still gone go with me in the morning?" he asked.

"Yeah, Nitro. I'll see you at nine a.m.," I said.

"Aite," he said and hung up the phone.

I grabbed the bag from Wal-Mart and hurried into the bathroom to empty my bladder.

Holding the pregnancy test in disbelief, the tears wouldn't stop falling. I picked up the phone and called my home girl Denise. Denise was my girl best friend and also Dinero's younger sister.

"Yes bitch," Denise answered the phone.

"NiNi," I cried.

"What the hell is wrong Kyra?" Denise answered in a worried tone.

"It was positive; the fucking test was positive. What am I gone do?" I asked. I could hear Denise huffing in the phone.

"You're gone tell my brother that you're carrying his child, duh," Denise whispered.

"Dinero must be around. Why are you whispering?" I asked.

"Yeah, I just got up and walked out, and he's in there with that Tori chick," she said. I rolled my eyes.

"I can't tell him," I cried.

"Why not? It is his right. You sure it ain't Nitro's?" Denise asked.

"Yes, it's his. I'm literally like a month late, and I have only been with Nitro once, and that was two days ago," I said.

"Well girl, I won't say anything, but you need to talk to my brother. I'm slick happy for y'all. Maybe now y'all will both stop playing and make it official hell." Denise laughed.

"Girl, hush. I'll hit you later. I got to sleep on this shit," I said.

"Aite then, girl," Denise said, and we both hung up the phone.

I sat there on the bed staring off into space; maybe just maybe Denise was right. I'll talk to Dinero tomorrow.

Dínero

Kyra was my entire heart. A nigga hated she was involved with Nitro. I ain't throwing salt, but shit, it's a fucked up feeling when the one you love is with someone else. Honestly, I think the only reason Kyra hooked up with Nitro was because of what all he could offer her. I don't think she loved him. Kyra didn't know, but I knew because she told my sister that she felt I settled for what I did and that a nigga didn't want more out of life. With me, everything is about timing. A nigga had plenty of money, but I wasn't able to touch that shit and get my hands dirty until my cousin fully retired from the streets. My cousin is Kyng St. Clair of the St. Clair Cartel. The day he stepped down, I can take over. All I needed was a partner. Everything should be done with precision. I just wished Kyra would've waited on a nigga. One day she would be mine and we gone run these streets together.

A nigga had an ok life growing up. My pops was Haitian, and my mom met him when she first moved to Nashville. They fell in love instantly, and then I was born. Shortly after my pops got heavy in the streets and ma was pregnant with my little sis Denise is when my father was murdered on the steps of our old house. That's when we moved where we stay now, and my mom and Kyra's mom became close friends.

I sat in the living room waiting on Tori to come through. I met her at this little hookah spot I be going to. Shorty had a banging ass body. I invited her over for a little Netflix and chill. Hell, I was still a nigga, and a nigga had needs.

Chapter 2

Kyra

The next morning, I was up bright and early waiting on Nitro to bring his ass. I barely slept a wink last night due to me tossing and turning. I was sitting at the kitchen table sipping on some green tea. My father walked in the kitchen, and I knew he was about to head out for work. He took care of home and mama didn't have to do shit but be domesticated. That's the one thing I admired about my parents they were still together. They had been together since high school. They barely argued. I don't know the secret, but they seem to be so perfect.

"Morning, sweetie," my father said, kissing me on my forehead.

"Hey dad," I said, fixing him a cup of coffee.

"What are you doing up so early?" he asked.

"I have to help a friend this morning," I said.

"Oh, you okay? You seem to be lost in thought when I walked in," my father said.

"Yes, I'm fine just a little tired that's all." My phone beeped, and I looked down at the text from Nitro stating that he was outside.

"I'll see you later, dad," I said, kissing him and heading out the door.

Nitro was parked in my driveway in a raggedy ass Dodge Neon. This wasn't his regular ride, so I knew he could tell by the look on my face that he had some explaining to do. As I was about to get in, I heard laughing coming from Dinero's yard, and I looked over to see him walking Tori out to her car. *This bitch had to spend the night,* I said to myself. We locked eyes, and I knew he knew I was hurt because the look on my face probably said it all. I felt myself getting sick to the stomach, so I hurried and got in the car with Nitro.

"Sup baby," Nitro said, leaning over to kiss me once I got in.

"Hey," I said really trying to hide my irritation.

"Damn, what's wrong with you?" he asked.

"Nothing baby, I'm just tired," I said quickly. I knew right then and there that I had to shake Dinero. Nitro pulled out, and I laid my head back on the seat and closed my eyes.

* * *

WHOOP! WHOOP!

The sound of police sirens woke me up, and I turned around. We were getting pulled over. "What's going on?" I asked Nitro.

"I don't know just be cool," he said, looking in the rearview. I looked down at my purse and noticed it was slightly opened, and I saw a few baggies inside of what looked to be weed and cocaine.

"What the fuck is this, Nitro?" I yelled.

"Please Kyra, just be calm. I can't get caught with no shit on me. I will never see the light of day again. They won't check you because you're a female. Just be cool. I got you," Nitro pleaded.

I sucked my teeth because now I was pissed the fuck off. It was two cops walking up to the car, one on my side and one on Nitro's side. Nitro rolled the window down.

"License and registration please," the officer asked. The other cop just stood by my window.

"What seems to be the problem officer?" Nitro asked while giving him his license.

"This vehicle was reported in a crime. Can you please step out the vehicle?" the officer asked.

The other officer opened my door and asked me to step out the car. Not thinking and letting my nerves get the best of me, I stepped out and left my purse on the seat. The officers searched the car. Nitro was sitting on the ground with his hands cuffed behind his back, and I stood there with my arms crossed shaking like a stripper.

"What do we have here?" The officer held up the bags that were in my purse. I looked at Nitro, and he looked at me with pleading eyes.

"It's mine," I said above a whisper. The officer shook his head and stood in my face "You're really willing to take the wrap for this piece of shit young lady?" I ignored the officer while the other officer slapped the cuffs on my wrist. Here I was pregnant and going to jail.

Release Day: A year and six months later.

Today was the day I had been waiting on, my release day back into the free world as a free woman. I had served a year and six months for that nigga Nitro. He only ended up doing a month. What kind of shit was that? He wrote me consistently saying how good things would be when I got out and how he loved me and I was his ride or die. My parents were pissed they didn't speak to me the first two months I was locked in here. Once I told them I was pregnant, they came around. Eight months in, I gave birth to a baby girl Dinelle. They had been raising my daughter and keeping my secret from Dinero. Dinero was mad that I took a charge for Nitro, but he came around, and he continued to be the best friend I knew he was. He sent letters and added money on my commissary. He tried to visit, but I refused visits from everyone except my parents. I walked outside the gate, and there stood my girl Denise. We ran to each other.

"Oh my god, I missed you Ky!" she yelled.

"Girl, look at you. Jail done filled you out and your hair so damn long now," she said going on and on.

"I know right, and I thank Dinelle for these curves, girl," I said.

"Speaking of which, you know Dinero saw your ma at the store the other day with her, and he was asking a million questions. I don't know what your ma told him, but he came home asking me. I played dumb, but I'm just warning you in case he comes to you," Denise said.

I nodded my head, and we got in the car. "I'm gone tell him. I know he gone be pissed and never speak to me again. Hell, Nitro doesn't even know. He gone know I was fucking around on him," I said just shaking my head at this whole damn mess.

"Um, you know Nitro and Dinero are partners now?" Denise said hesitantly. I looked at Denise.

"What the fuck you mean partners?" I asked. "Business wise, they got the streets on lock working under Kyng. Dinero had a connect through our cousin, and he needed a partner, so he hooked up with Nitro. I hate to say it but bitch my brother ain't settling no more," Denise said.

"This shit can't be happening," I said.

"Enough about them niggas. Girl, when you get home, there is some clothes and shit in your room. You got a party to hit up tonight. Go wash that jail funk off you and get right for tonight. I'll be to scoop you at ten." Denise said, pulling up my parents' home.

"Thanks, girl," I said. I got out the car looking at my home. I missed this place, and it felt good to be home.

I walked into the house and was greeted by my parents and a smiling Dinelle. I grabbed my baby and planted a million kisses on her.

"Mommy missed you so much," I cried. Dinelle was ten months old, and she looked just like Dinero. I hugged my parents and apologized to them.

"I thank you guys so much for helping me with her, I owe y'all," I said.

"Girl, we did what any parent would do, now that you got this child, you got to make better decisions for your life. You need to tell Dinero that's his child, even though I think he has a feeling after our run in we had the other day. You owe it to him; don't let him miss out on any more of her life," my mother told me.

"Yes ma'am, I plan on telling him. I'm gone take a shower and get out of these clothes," I said, handing Dinelle to my mother.

As I walked into my bedroom, I smiled at how my parents had Dinelle's side fixed up. I looked on the bed and saw the bags of clothes Denise left. I smiled; she had looked out for me on the clothes. I walked into my bathroom and started my shower. Washing off all the jail filth, it felt like if I scrubbed my skin any harder, it was gone fall off. I stood there until the water turned cold. Turning off the shower and stepping out, I stood in the mirror and dried my hair. I applied some leave in conditioner and let my hair air dry. Stepping back in my room, I grabbed a pair of legging and a long sleeve crop top sweater that showed my belly. Even though I had Dinelle, my stomach was flat as a board. I threw on a pair of UGG's and headed downstairs with my parents and Dinelle.

My parents were in the kitchen laughing and talking, and I reached into the playpen and grabbed Dinelle.

“Hey fat mama,” I said. I sat on the couch and held my daughter. I knew I needed to talk to Dinero as soon as possible. I needed to get me a phone in the morning. I was interrupted by a knock at the door.

“I’ll get it!” I yelled at my parents. I opened the door, and there stood Dinero. This nigga had always been fine, but I could tell he was that nigga now; he looked like money. He stood there 6’2. He had gotten bigger, so he looked to be about a good 200 something pounds. He had an iced-out bottom grill. His dark chocolate skin made the ice pop out.

“Oh, hey, Dinero,” I said. He nodded his head and stepped in

“Welcome home, Ky,” he said not as excited as I hoped it would be. As he walked by, his fragrance of whatever cologne he wore played tricks with my nose.

“Can we go somewhere and talk?” he asked.

“Sure. Ma, can you grab her while we go talk?” I asked.

“No, bring her,” he said. Mama gave me a head nod like it’s time.

“Ok, come on,” I said as we headed upstairs. I could feel him staring a hole in me from behind. We walked in my room, and I placed Dinelle in her crib. Dinero came right after me and picked her up.

Dinero

I looked at this little girl who looked just like me. I knew this was my child the first time I saw her. I had mixed emotions. I was angry with Kyra for keeping this a secret. I was happy because we had created a baby out of love. This shit was just complicated. I turned to face Kyra and damn she looked good. She wasn't the little Kyra that I once knew. Jail and this baby had baby girl looking like a whole damn meal.

"Why come you didn't tell me about my daughter?" I asked Kyra. Kyra sat down on the bed.

"I was going to tell you eventually. I just didn't when I should have. I had planned on telling you the day I got arrested, but things and my emotions just wouldn't allow me," she said.

'Dammit Kyra, I've missed ten whole months of my daughter life. As much as we talked while you were gone, you couldn't tell a nigga he was a daddy?" I asked not trying to raise my voice.

Kyra looked sad, and I know she meant well, but this was some fucked up shit. "Now I got to tell Tori this shit, and what you think yo nigga gone say, you know we fuck with each other tough now," I said. Kyra stood and crossed her arms.

"Oh, why you got to tell Tori anything? I get it now, y'all together ain't y'all?" Kyra asked.

I could tell by the way her voice cracked she was hurt. I had kept that a secret from her the whole time she was locked up. Tori was my girl. She filled a void while Kyra was away, but deep down no one could ever replace what I felt for Kyra. She was who I wanted and where my heart belonged, and now that she birthed my daughter I wanted to wife her. That shit sounded good in my head, but I knew shit was complicated as hell.

"Look, yeah I'm with Tori. I should've told you, but I didn't." I said, placing Dinelle back in the crib.

I walked over to Kyra, and she held her head down. I lifted her head and looked into her eyes.

"Look, all bullshit aside, Ky. My heart is with you always has been and still is. Yeah, I'm pissed about you keeping the baby from me, but I got you and my shorty till I die. I don't want to lose you," I said. She looked up at me and smiled.

"I love you, ugly," she said and leaned in to kiss me when her room door flew open.

Chapter 3

Nitro

What's up I know y'all think a nigga ain't shit. My name Nathanial, but everyone calls me Nitro. Ain't too much to tell about me. I've been in these streets since I was eleven years old. I'm the only child. My mom left when I was born, causing me to be raised by my father. When I met Kyra, a nigga really didn't have no intentions of having a full relationship with shorty, but she drew a nigga in. She wasn't on no messy shit like the females be these days. The biggest turn on was that she was in college.

The day Kyra took that charge for me no questions asked, I knew I had a keeper. She was a rider. She didn't fold on a nigga like your average chick would do. Now that Kyra was home, I was gone give her everything she deserved and treat her like the queen she was. I was headed to East Nashville to Kyra's parent's house. Yeah, a nigga should've been there when she got out, but I had to take care of business and make sure the crib and shit was straight. My phone rang, and I hit the Bluetooth in the car to answer.

"What Tori?" I yelled.

"I been calling you since Dinero left, can we link up or not? I need to taste that dick again." I sighed this girl was a fucking trip. I mean a nigga can't fault her ass. I've been knocking her ass off for a minute behind Dinero back. Dinero thinks a nigga's blind to the fact of him and Kyra, but I been knowing about them. So why not help myself to his bitch.

"Look a nigga ain't got time for all that, I'm headed to get my woman and bring her home. What you need to worry about is how your nigga gone act now that his precious Kyra is home," I said.

"What Kyra is out?" Tori asked.

I chuckled. "Yep, so don't hit my line," I said, hanging up the phone.

I pulled up to Kyra's and what do you know, this nigga Dinero was already here. I grabbed the flowers that I had got and stepped out and headed to the door. I hit the lock on my 2017 Jaguar XF and was greeted by Kyra's mother, Mrs. Mitchell.

"Nathanial," she said.

She ain't like a nigga I could tell she had every right not to, but I always tried to keep her and Mr. Mitchell happy by throwing them money to cover expenses while Kyra was away.

"Hey, Mrs. Mitchell," I spoke walking into the house. "Kyra is upstairs with Dinero. You can wait down here." She said. "They're both expecting me, so I'm gone head on up," I said, lying and started skipping up the stairs.

I placed my ears to the door to see if I heard anything out of the ordinary. I'm tripping I thought and I opened the door to what looks like was about to be a kiss. Kyra looked as if she had been crying, and she ran to me.

“Nitro!” she said damn near jumping in my arms.

“Hey baby, sorry I couldn’t get here earlier. I had to get your surprise together,” I said.

Dinero dapped me up. “Sup nigga, why is everybody looking sad as fuck, what’s going on?” I asked.

Kyra spoke up first. “Well before anyone goes anywhere I have to break the news to you like I just did to Dinero,” she said.

A nigga was nervous. Kyra walked over to a baby crib that I didn’t even notice when I walked into the room and picked up a smiling little girl. My mouth got dry, and I felt anger.

“This bet not be my baby.” I said not even realizing I was pissed.

If this was my child and she kept this from me, I was liable to choke her ass. “Nitro, this is Dinelle, mine and Dinero’s daughter.” Kyra spoke. I looked at Dinero, and he nodded his head “I just found out myself, homie,” he said.

Kyra

"I was pregnant before me and you got together, well before we were ever intimate. I didn't know, and when I got locked up, I just kept it a secret," I said lying a little.

I wasn't about to tell Nitro everything. I didn't want to be with him anyways. I wanted to be with Dinero, but I had to play this shit by ear. Knowing that Dinero was still with Tori, I wasn't about to end shit with Nitro. Nitro looked like all his life had been sucked from him.

"Damn, that's fucked up. I mean shit I guess we all just one big ass family because I'm not gone stand in the way of my nigga taking care of his seed. So enough of the sulking, you are home now baby, and it's time you head to our new home," Nitro said.

I looked at him like he was crazy. "Our home?" I asked.

"Yeah, girl. You think I'm gone let my girl stay with her parents when she's got her own house and that bitch is too big for me to stay there all alone," Nitro said.

I glanced at Dinero who I could tell wasn't feeling the situation but was trying to front like he was.

"How about I take Dinelle to my mom's since she need to meet her grandchild and y'all handle what y'all need to handle. I will link up with y'all later at the party," Dinero said, grabbing Dinelle.

Dinero left out, and I looked at Nitro. I almost forgot how fine he was. Nitro favored Don off *Black Ink*.

"I missed you," I said laying it on thick. "So about this house, I'm ready when you are," I said. Nitro smiled and grabbed my hand.

"Come on girl," he said. I stopped to grab the bags off the bed that Denise had got me. "Leave that shit; you're getting everything new," Nitro said, pulling me out of the room.

* * *

Nitro and I pulled up to a two-story home in Whites Creek, TN in the Whites Creek Manor subdivision. I was speechless I had never seen a home so beautiful. I hopped out the car and ran up to the door.

"Oh my god, baby!" I yelled. Nitro smiled.

"I got another surprise for you," Nitro said, walking towards the two-car garage. He hit the remote, and the garage door opened. There sat a matching 2017 Jaguar XF in my favorite color.

"I told you I had you covered boo; I wasn't playing. Girl, I owe you the world, and I'm gone give it to you," Nitro said.

This made things more complicated now. Here Nitro was trying to make up for what he did, and all I wanted was to be with Dinero.

"Thank you, baby," I said.

I grabbed Nitro by the hands and led him into the house. I wore a devilish grin because I was about to put it on him something awful.

We barely made it in the bedroom, and I was all over Nitro. As much as I would've loved for this to be Dinero, I took what I could get. I pushed Nitro on the bed and undressed as he stared at me hungrily.

"Come sit on my face," Nitro demanded.

Like a naughty schoolgirl, I did what I was told. He started slurping on my pussy like it was his last meal. A few minutes after he went to work, he smacked my ass to let me know to get up, flipping me over, he pulled his shirt over his head and entered me from behind.

"Fuck!" I yelled out. I had forgotten how big Nitro's ass was.

"Damn girl," Nitro said.

The funny thing is that this was only me and Nitro's second time being intimate. I know this nigga been fuckin' somebody while I was away. I was starting to get angry, so I pretended that I was about to climax. I started bucking faster and throwing it back being all loud and shit.

"I'm bout to cum," I said. Nitro sped up.

"Pull out," I said. Nitro continued pumping then released inside of me. "What the fuck Nitro, I said pull out," I said, getting up pissed the fuck off. '

"Pull out for what, you're my girl. Oh, so you can give Dinero a baby, but you don't want to have mine?" he asked.

I rolled my eyes ‘What the fuck ever. Nigga, I just came home and got to make up to my child what I missed first before I decide I want to throw another child into the mix,” I said, starting the shower.

“I’m tripping, forgive me?” Nitro asked. I pulled him into the shower with me.

Chapter 4

Tori

"What the fuck you mean you got a daughter with this bitch?" I yelled at Dinero. He had just told me the news that Kyra had his daughter and kept it a secret.

"I mean what kind of woman hides a child from a nigga," I said, putting my makeup on in the mirror. Dinero walked into the bathroom and stood behind me looking at me in the mirror.

"First off, watch your fucking mouth. Kyra, ain't did shit to you, so calling her out her name is uncalled for," he said through gritted teeth.

Did this nigga just defend this bitch, now I see what Nitro be talking about. I stopped doing my eyebrows.

"Who the fuck is your woman? Me or Kyra?" I asked. Dinero rolled his eyes

"Man here you go starting all this unnecessary shit, Tori. Kyra is a part of my life and now the mother of my child. I won't tolerate anyone disrespecting you or her. I'm with you, but you also need to get used to my daughter being around," he said.

"I don't have a problem with your daughter, but Kyra needs to know her place?" I said. Dinero turned around.

“What the fuck are you talking about? Kyra ain’t worried about me. She knows about us, and she is Nitro’s girl, always has been,” Dinero said.

“Apparently not if you got a baby with her,” I said, slamming the door to the bathroom while I finished beating my face.

Dinero

Man, Tori was about to work my fucking nerves. Why all of sudden she so worried about Kyra. I guess she had every reason to be worried because since I left Kyra’s, she and Dinelle was the only thing on my mind. Shit didn’t sit well with me her being with Nitro, but it is what it is. I called Denise to see if everything was coming along with Kyra’s welcome home party. I really had paid for the entire thing, but I told Denise to pretend she was doing it. Tori walked out looking sexy as shit. Now, I wasn’t no bum ass nigga, so every bitch I touch looked bad as fuck. Tori wasn’t no all-natural chick body wise like Kyra, but it wasn’t outrageous. She admitted to an ass and titty job when we met. She was one for her inches as y’all girls call that shit. She was a redbone, unlike Kyra.

Kyra had been blessed with ass and titties. She was peanut butter brown and had a set of hazel eyes that a nigga would fall weak for every time. Kyra’s hair came to the middle of her back; she had to have some Indian somewhere in her bloodline.

“You ready?” Tori asked, knocking me out my thoughts.
“Yeah come on,” I said as we exited my crib.

Tori was in the passenger seat. I could tell she still was a little salty from today's events. I reached over and grabbed her hand, and she looked at me

"What?" she asked smiling.

"I just don't want you to be mad, baby," I said.

"I'm good. I ain't tripping," she said. I nodded and turned the radio up.

Kyra

We pulled up at Agenda, and the crowd was lit. I was glad to be home. Nitro walked around and opened the door, and I stepped out feeling like royalty.

"Goddamn girl, don't make me hurt no nigga in here tonight looking all fine and shit," Nitro said. I giggled.

I wore a Versace pierced leather jacket, and a pair of Versace studded skinny jeans on my feet were a pair of Manolo Blahnik Isola Brocade bootie boots. I felt like that bitch at the moment. Nitro was matching my fly rocking his Versace leather jacket and pants with shoes to match. We were about to walk into the VIP line when out of my peripheral, I saw Dinero and this Tori chick walking up hand in hand. This Barbie looking bitch. What does he see in her?

Dinero walked up and dapped up Nitro and Tori hugged Nitro, and I wasn't feeling that shit either. Dinero hit me with a one-armed hug.

"Kyra, I want you to meet my girl Tori," he said.

Tori held her hand out for me to shake. I don't know what came over me, but I was not about to shake this bitch's hand. The silence was awkward, and Dinero gave me that same damn look Nitro gave me when I got arrested. I finally said, "Hey." That's all I could muster up.

"I just want you to know that I will treat your daughter like she is my own," Tori said.

I don't know if anybody else caught it, but this bitch was giving me a sarcastically salty vibe. Denise came and grabbed me.

"Hey girl come on," she said, pulling me through the door.

"You saved me. Girl, I felt myself about to pop off on Tori. Her vibe ain't coinciding with mine. Plus, I hate having to be fake," I told Denise.

"Girl I know, that's why I ran over there. Look just enjoy yourself tonight and try not to let her or my big head ass brother ruin your night," Denise said.

I followed her to our booth, and the bottle popping had started.

The night was going good, even though every time I looked up, I saw that Tori bitch looking at me. I know I wasn't tripping, but I could've sworn I saw her wink at Nitro. I was feeling the liquor; we were on our third bottle of Hennessy.

"You good?" Denise leaned over and asked me.

“Hell yeah,” I said.

Nitro and Dinero were at the edge of our section turned up with bottles in hand, and Dinero looked back over his shoulder, and we locked eyes.

“Y’all ain’t slick,” Denise said.

“Girl, shut up.”

The DJ switched the music up and started playing some old school throwback music. I knew God was messing with me because mine and Dinero’s song came on

“Sleepless nights and lonely days are all that fill my head all of the time, oh baby. But all I do is think about the way you make me feel because, baby, this love is so real. Soon as I get home, I’ll make it up to you baby I’ll do what I gotta do.”

I sang along with so much emphasis not even realizing I was standing on the couch in the VIP section using the Hennessy bottle as a microphone.

“Bitch, this shit going on Snapchat!” Denise yelled.

Dinero was just standing there nodding along. Everything was fine until Tori stood her ass up and went over to Dinero pulling him in for a kiss. I instantly got sick hopping down off the couch and speed walking out of our section bumping past Dinero and Tori.

I made it to the bathroom and Denise was right behind me. “Girl, you aite?” she asked.

I ran into a stall and threw up everything from that night. I stood up and had to shake my thoughts. Coming out the stall, Denise and Nitro was standing in the bathroom.

"Nitro, what are you doing in here?" I asked, walking over to the sink to rinse my mouth out.

"Checking on your drunk ass." Nitro laughed. I shook my head.

"I'm good I'm gone go stand outside for a little bit, Denise can you come with me?" I asked. "Yeah girl, come on," Denise said, leading me outside to the patio area.

Sitting outside sipping on a bottle of water, Denise was cracking up at me, but I didn't see anything funny.

"You good?" I heard Dinero voice before I saw him. Turning around, I rolled my eyes.

"Yeah I'm straight," I lied.

"Fuck no, she drunk and in her feelings," Denise said.

"Bitch," I said.

"What? Stop playing. It ain't nobody out here but us. Y'all play too many games for me. Your ass ain't stuttin' Tori and Kyra you sholl in the hell ain't stuttin' Nitro. Y'all need to be together for Dinelle," Denise rambled. Dinero shook his head.

"Look, did you get hooked up with a cell yet?" Dinero asked me.

"Yeah, why?" I answered.

"I'm gone get your number from NiNi tomorrow and hit you up so we can spend some time together," Dinero said.

"Here comes yo bitch," I said, nodding at Tori walking over here looking stank faced.

"This why I couldn't find you, you out here all in her face," Tori said.

I chuckled and looked at Denise, "She mad ain't she?" I stood to walk away when Tori stepped in front of me

"Don't think because y'all have a child together you gone be sinking yo claws in my man." This bitch was bold

"Question of the day. Is that your man, sis? I promise you; you should be very worried," I said, using my arm to move this bitch out my way.

Her mouth flew open, and I could hear her and Dinero going at it while I walked back to find Nitro. I was ready to go.

Chapter 5

Kyra

The next day I woke up with a splitting headache. I rolled over, and Nitro was snoring his ass off. I threw the covers back and placed my feet on the floor. Running my fingers through my hair, I stood up and headed to the bathroom. I looked around and found me a BC powder then headed to the kitchen. Last night I was so caught up in fucking and surprises I didn't really get to take in how huge our house was, and how beautiful everything was. I smiled walking over to the fridge I opened it and grabbed me something to take this BC powder with. After throwing it back, I headed back upstairs and heard Nitro's phone going off. I walked over to his side of the bed and glanced at his phone. I picked it up.

T: I need to see you, or I'm gone confront your bitch.

I held the phone in my hand and instantly got pissed. But why the hell was I mad? I could use this to call it off and be with Dinero. I took the water I was holding in my hand and poured it on Nitro.

"What the fuck, Kyra?" He jumped up.

"Who the fuck is T and tell that bitch I said she could have your ass," I said, throwing his phone at him.

"What?" he said, picking up the phone. "Man, this shit ain't nothing, ain't nobody messing around, shit."

I walked over to the closet and started looking for me something to wear. "I know your ass was fucking somebody while I was locked up nigga. Keep fucking with me and next time I go to jail it's gone be for my own damn charges!" I yelled. Nitro stormed into the closet.

"You need to chill the fuck out. Yeah, a nigga had sex with other bitches while you were gone, but that's just what it was. Nothing more nothing less," Nitro said.

"Whatever," I said not really trying to hear shit he was saying. I hurried to the bathroom and showered.

Nitro

I was gone smack the shit out of Tori for texting my phone. That bitch was becoming reckless. Kyra was walking around this bitch with a damn chip on her shoulder now. She can cool her ass off because she ain't going nowhere. I walked in the living room

"What you got planned for the day?" I asked.

Kyra was changing purses. She sucked her teeth before answering. "Probably go meet up with this bitch T," she answered being smart.

"Yo smart ass mouth," I said handing her a wad of money "Just so you won't be walking round broke. I got some moves to make, so I'll see you later," I said, giving her a quick peck on the cheek.

I hopped in my ride and peeled out. I dialed Tori ass.

"Hello," she answered.

"You must be dying for a nigga to knock yo yella ass out, huh?" I yelled. Shorty had me pissed off.

"Oh, so now it's a problem because Kyra's ass out?" Tori said.

"Bitch, you damn right it's a fucking problem. Kyra is my motherfucking woman. I call your ass when I want some pussy and you threatening me is just gone get you cut off!" I yelled.

"Meet me at my spot in Midtown," I said, hanging up the phone.

I called Kyra, and just like I figured she didn't pick up. Pulling up at my spot, I looked around to see if I saw Tori car or not. The only person that knew about this place was Dinero. This was my stash spot. I parked my whip and hopped out, heading towards the door.

I walked into the house and no soon as I was about to close the door, I heard Tori calling out, "Hold up!"

I stood in the door waiting for her to come in. "I knew you missed me," she said. I jacked her up by her coat collar in the air

"Let me tell your ass something and you listen good. Keep trying to do some slick shit to break my girl and me up, and I promise you your mammy gone be rocking that black dress sooner than anticipated," I said, throwing her ass on the couch.

"Nigga, you're the one started this shit. I'm telling your ass now you better watch Dinero because they were looking mighty cozy outside last night when she went outside," Tori said.

"Look you worry about your nigga, and I'll worry about my damn woman. Now suck my dick before I change my damn mind," I said, forcing her head towards my dick.

Dinero

A nigga was headed to Kyra's parents' house to scoop her up. I didn't think she was gone call a nigga. I thought my sis was lying when she said Ky had called her asking for my number. I told her she ain't have to pack shit we were finna shoot to Memphis for a quick little trip. I pulled into my mom's driveway. She and Kyra's mom had taken Dinelle shopping for church tomorrow. I shot Kyra a text letting her know I was outside. About five minutes later, Kyra came strolling outside looking like she was on the cover of *Vogue*. I hit the lock to unlock the door as she climbed in.

"Wassup, baby daddy!" she said, laughing.

"Who would've thought," I said and pulled off heading to Memphis.

Our ride to Memphis was like old times we were able to talk about everything from her experience in jail, her pregnancy with Dinelle, even how she was pissed at Nitro for fucking off on her while locked up, and how some chick texted him this morning. Hearing her angry about that kind of had a nigga thinking. Why was she mad when she said she was looking for a way out anyway? My cell rung, and I answered it on Bluetooth.

"Hello," I said.

"Where are you?" Tori's voice boomed through the speaker, causing Kyra to wake up.

"On my way to Memphis, had to make a run. I'll be back sometime in the morning," I said quickly. Kyra chuckled and closed her eyes.

"Damn Dinero, you could've told me sooner," Tori whined.

"Girl bye, I got somebody on the other line," I said, hanging up in her face.

"You ain't have to hang up because I was in here," Kyra said.
"She would've been hounding a nigga," I said.

"So, we gone just keep playing games when it's obvious we both don't want to be with the people we with?" Kyra asked in a more serious tone.

I knew this would come up. The only reason why I was sticking around was because couple weeks ago I found a positive pregnancy test in the trash and I was waiting on her to tell me the news. I didn't want to leave her if she was indeed pregnant.

"In due time," I responded to Kyra. She rolled her eyes and looked out the window.

We arrived at The Westin Memphis and headed to our room to get cleaned up for dinner. I had gone into the bathroom to take a shower while Kyra was talking to her mom checking on our daughter. Stepping out the shower, I heard Kyra sound as if she was arguing with someone.

"Nitro, I'm not finna tell your ass a damn thing. Don't be worrying about where I am you worry about that bitch T texting your phone. It doesn't matter, nigga. I figured you were getting your dick wet anyways, I'm not even fucked up with that. My problem is you not letting these hoes know your woman is home, and that shit is dead. I'll be home in the morning I'm staying over here at mama's and going to church in the morning," she rambled on.

I stepped in the room making my presence known with my towel wrapped around my waist.

"I love you too," Kyra said and ended her call.

Kyra

Dinero stood there looking at me like I was crazy "Damn so you really gone tell that nigga that while I'm standing here?" Dinero asked.

I stood and walked over to him.

"Chill, I had to tell him back. You know I love you and only you, even though it's clear you're playing games," I told him.

"Ky, nobody's playing games with you ma. I can't tell you right now because I don't have all the info, but it's a reason why I can't just end things right now. But look, I brought you here so we could enjoy each other company like we need to," Dinero said.

I grabbed his towel and removed it from around his waist. That big boy popped up and greeted me. I got on my knees and locked eyes with Dinero. Taking all ten inches in my mouth to his shit was invisible. I made sure I got it hella wet and lifted it up and hummed on his balls.

"Fuck girl!" Dinero yelled out. I continue to suck him off until he literally pulled me up and threw me on the bed.

"You tryna have a nigga in here singing and shit. Now it's my turn to make you sing," he said, entering me from behind. Dinero's dick was huge and fat. Nitro wasn't bad, but I was made for Dinero.

"Fuck this pussy," I said, looking back over my shoulders and biting my bottom lip. Dinero was pounding the fuck out of my shit. He pulled out, and I felt his tongue glide across my pussy lips and then my asshole. Dinero went to work on my pussy I just hope he was ready because I was about to drown his ass. He smacked my ass.

"Girl, I'm bout to cum," he said. I swear I was about to climax myself so my judgment was cloudy until I felt him speed up.

"Pull out, I'm not on birth control," I said.

"Too late." Dinero laughed and rolled over.

We both laid there tapped out when Dinero phone started ringing. He reached over to the nightstand and grabbed his phone.

"Yeah, what's up?" I heard a male voice, and it sounded like Nitro.

"Yeah I came on a run, but not no run for what we got going on. I'm looking at some property. Yeah. Aite I'll hit you when I get back," Dinero said and hung up the phone. He looked angry, and his jaws were twitching

"What's wrong?" Dinero looked at his phone.

"This nigga Nitro asked me why I'm making a run in Memphis without him," Dinero said.

"Ok, so what's the problem, that's the excuse you were using, right?" I asked with a confused look on my face. Dinero looked at me.

"The only person I told that shit to was Tori," he said.

"Oh, maybe he called Tori looking for you, and she told him." He pulled up something on his phone and whatever he was looking at pissed him off even more.

"This bitch at the stash spot in Midtown. What the fuck she doing there, and apparently with Nitro?" Dinero yelled. By now I was interested in whatever was going on.

"What you thinking, Dinero? And how you know where she at?" I asked.

"Her phone."

Dinero dialed Tori number putting her on speakerphone and waited for her to answer. "Yeah, where you at?" he asked.

"Meeting Nitro, dropping off the money you left for him. He said he needed it, but you had left town," Tori said. I caught the smile that graced his face after she said that as if it was a sigh of relief.

"You right, my bad I forgot all about that. Good looking out," Dinero said.

I rolled my eyes and headed to the bathroom to clean off. This gone be harder than I thought. He not about to break up with Tori no time soon. This whole little time we've been in Memphis Nitro and Tori ass been in our mix. I was stepping out the shower, and Dinero stood there leaned against the bathroom entrance.

"You looked relieved that your girlfriend wasn't cheating on you," I said sarcastically. I walked over to the sink and grabbed a toothbrush out the bag to brush my teeth.

"I mean you got to understand a nigga do got some feelings for her. We have been together for a year and some change. I know you don't like that shit, but a nigga's sorry," Dinero said. "You still gone fuck with a nigga, right?" he asked.

I looked at him, and his looks alone was making me weak. I told him that Nas was his daddy because he was identical to him.

“Do you think I should continue cheating on my man just because you want leave your girl?” I asked. Dinero rubbed his hands over his head

“I mean come on Ky, you know a nigga wants to be with you though. Shit ain’t that easy, and you know it. I thought you would be happy a nigga’s tryna spend some time with you and shit,” Dinero said, sounding agitated.

“I’m hungry, and I can’t think on no empty stomach. Might as well enjoy this trip while we can just in case it won’t happen again,” I said, walking past him.

Chapter 6

Kyra

Since our Memphis trip things have been so off between Dinero and I. Time with him had become scarce as far as us having alone time with each other, and Nitro and I had become closer. Dinero was spending a lot of time with Dinelle; he was wearing the father name well. Denise and I were at Opry Mills Mall getting some things.

"Have you talked to my brother about anything else besides Dinelle?" she asked.

"Nope and, why should I? I'm not about to chase his ass. I think I'm gone try to stick it out with Nitro; things have been good between us," I said.

"Ugh girl I don't even think you believe yourself with that one," Denise said.

"I mean what's wrong with him? Y'all ain't liked us together since day one?" I asked.

"It's not him it's the shit he did that got you locked up that everyone is mad about. But if you're happy then ain't no point in speaking on it," Denise said, walking into Victoria Secret.

We were grabbing some bra and panty sets when I heard her voice.

"Hey, Denise!" Tori said. I rolled my eyes and continued to look at the bras.

"Aw, hey Tori," Denise said.

"Girl these titties done got huge on me in the past couple of weeks," Tori said as if anybody was paying attention to her.

"Denise, can you make me some of your banana pudding, please. I've been craving it something awful," Tori said. My ears perked up, and Denise turned around.

"Tori, what are you rambling on about? As you can see we are trying to shop," Denise said clearly irritated with Tori's presence. I laughed, and Tori turned to me as if she wanted to say something.

"Anyways let me finish telling you about that trip to Memphis," I told Denise, walking off leaving Tori to marinate on that.

"Bitch, you is childish." Denise laughed.

Dinero

Nitro and I had just wrapped up our meeting with Kyng. We were about to get a shipment of guns to come through. Shit was looking good on our end. We were bringing in a hefty amount of money.

"You good, nigga?" Nitro asked. We were at Kyng's house chilling playing the game.

"Man, I think Tori's pregnant, but she ain't said nothing to a nigga yet."

Nitro damn near choked. “My bad, bruh,” he said, hitting his chest. “So how you figure she’s pregnant?” Nitro asked. “I found a positive pregnancy test in the trash,” Dinero said, hitting the blunt and passing it to me.

“It could’ve been somebody else’s. I wish Kyra ass hurry up and get pregnant a nigga been putting in work trying to get a baby in her,” Nitro said, causing me to get antsy.

Nitro’s phone went off he looked at it and silenced his phone. “I swear this nagging ass bitch won’t leave me alone!” Nitro yelled out.

“Don’t let Kyra’s crazy ass find out.” I chuckled.

Tori

I had called Nitro to fill him in on the little shit I just heard. I can’t help but to think the petty bitch was trying throw hints mentioning Memphis and shit. Fuck! I hated Kyra. This bitch was like a thorn in my fucking side. She doesn’t deserve Dinero nor Nitro. I was sitting in the living room thinking about how I could bring this bitch down. I just don’t know for sure if she’s fucking Dinero, but if I put it out there, Nitro will start looking. An evil smile crept on my face, and I was just about to call Nitro back when I heard keys jiggling in the lock. Dinero walked in.

“Hey boo,” I said, standing up to greet him. He kissed me on the lips.

"Sit down we need to talk, Tori," he said. From the vibe he was giving off, I was getting worried

"What's up?" I said.

"You pregnant?" he asked. My mouth flew open. Instead of answering right away, my mind started racing. "Hello? Are you pregnant, Tori?" Dinero asked me again. I snapped out of the daze I was in and cocked my head to the side.

"No, why would you ask me that?" I asked.

"I found a positive pregnancy test in the trash," Dinero said. *Fuck!* I thought.

"Dinero, for one that was not my test; Kesha came over here and took it. Two, if I was pregnant don't you think I would've told you by now," I said, letting the lies just flow freely from my mouth.

The truth was that was my test, and I was pregnant, but I was getting a damn abortion. I really wanted this baby bad, but I knew it wasn't Dinero baby. I was carrying Nitro's child. I could tell by the look on Dinero face he was skeptical. "Yeah aite, Tori," he said, walking away heading into the kitchen.

I needed to talk to Nitro ASAP.

Nitro

Kyra had walked in with Dinelle.

"Nitro, can you go get some of the bags out of the car, please?" she asked, putting Dinelle down on the living room floor.

"Bags? Kyra, you done went and bought the mall again?" I said, getting up removing myself from the couch.

"I had to get everything for Dinelle's birthday and her party." She laughed heading to the bathroom.

I headed outside to the car and started grabbing bags out of the back seat when my phone rang. Looking at the phone, it was Tori.

"Yeah," I answered.

"Nitro we need to talk," she said.

"We sholl do, what's this I hear about you being pregnant?" I asked, looking back over my shoulder to make sure Kyra wasn't creeping up on a nigga.

"I am, but I need money for an abortion," Tori said.

"An abortion, shorty you got a whole nigga. So, I'm assuming you're saying this is my baby? A nigga can't have no shit like this getting out because if Kyra finds out, she's gone kick your ass and mine," I said.

"Fuck Kyra, you gone give me the money or what?" she asked.

"If Kyra finds out what? What is it that if I find out about I'm kicking ass?" Kyra said, startling the fuck out of me. I hung the phone up.

“Um, baby,” I said.

“Don’t fucking baby me. Nitro, what the fuck you got going on?” Kyra said, running up on me, causing to drop the bags and my phone. Kyra reached down, grabbed my phone, and ran in the house.

Kyra

I walked outside to help Nitro get the bags out my car, and I walk in on the end of him saying something like if I find out about something I’m gone kick his ass and somebodies else ass. I had grabbed Nitro phone and ran into the house locking myself in the bathroom. I unlocked his phone and went to the last call. It said T. Oh, ok this little bitch again. Nitro banged on the door.

“Kyra, open this fucking door right now!” he yelled.

“Fuck you, Nitro!” I yelled back. I press call on the phone.

“Damn, you hung up on me. It’s like that. You gone give me the money or not?” this bitch said. I couldn’t catch her voice, but this bitch sounded hella familiar.

“Bitch, why you keep calling my man phone?” I yelled. This bitch started laughing.

“Nobody wants your man, but I do need this money for an abortion,” the girl said. I felt the rage building up in me. Nitro finally came busting through the door

“Bitch, give me my fucking phone!” he yelled, snatching the phone from my hands.

I started throwing blows at his face because now he had me all the way fucked up. "Fuck you Nitro, I ain't never liked your ass!" I yelled still throwing blows.

SMACK!

My head flew back, and I felt my face stinging. Holding my face, I looked at Nitro.

"I ain't never liked your ass either; you were just a duck ass bitch that I was using anyway," Nitro said.

I ran out of the bathroom and started grabbing my things.

"Where you think you're going? You think I'm about to let you leave here so you can run to that nigga Dinero and tell him I hit you. Nah, you gone chill out here for a little bit. Fuck you thought?" Nitro said.

"So, you got some other bitch pregnant?" I asked. For some reason, I was hurt. Nitro sighed and put his hands in his pockets

"Look, Kyra; I'm gone handle that. I haven't even been fucking with that bitch, but I am gone give her the money for the abortion," Nitro said.

Dinelle cries caused me to head downstairs and check on my daughter. I grabbed Dinelle and sat on the couch. I had nothing to say to Nitro, now that I knew how he really felt about me. I knew we both hated each other, but leaving him wouldn't be easy. If I could be with Dinero, I would be with him forever.

Chapter 7

Dinero

It had been two weeks since I saw Dinelle and Kyra. Kyra said her and Dinelle were getting over a cold. Today was Dinelle's birthday, so I was excited to be able to see my daughter and Kyra. Tori and I were in the car heading to East Park Center where we had rented out a space for Dinelle party. It was a beautiful May day, not too hot with a slight breeze. I don't know why I even brought her because her attitude was off.

"Before we get in here you need to get your attitude together," I looked over at Tori and told her. She rolled her eyes.

"Yes sir, daddy," she replied sarcastically. I shook my head and parked my whip. I stepped out of my 2017 Bentley Continental and hit the lock. Walking into the center, I loved how Denise had everything set up. That's one thing I can say about my sister; she took her party planning to another level. That's exactly why I gave her the money to start her business. Tori went and sat down in the back corner with her face glued to her phone. I swear I was sick of this bitch. I walked over to Dinelle.

"Hey, baby girl," I said, kissing her. I walked over to Mr. and Mrs. Mitchell. "Hey y'all, have y'all seen Kyra?" I asked.

"Yeah, she went to the bathroom," Mr. Mitchell said.

"Thanks, pops," I said, dapping him up.

I looked over at Tori, and she was still sitting with her lips stuck out. I walked down the hall and knocked on the bathroom door. I looked around, and the coast was clear, so I stepped in the women's bathroom. Kyra was standing in the mirror applying makeup, which I found odd because Kyra's skin was flawless and she never wore makeup.

"What you doing?" I said, startling her.

"What are you doing in here, Dinero?" she said, placing the makeup back in her purse. I grabbed her face and noticed a little dark spot on her cheek.

"What happen to your face?" I asked.

"Nothing, it's just a pimple I popped that left a scar," she said, walking past me.

"Damn, what's up though, Ky? You've been standoffish as fuck." She turned and faced me.

"Nothing. I'm cool, Dinero," she said, walking out the bathroom.

I stood there for a few moments before I decided to step out. I linked back up with Kyra, and we started the birthday party for our daughter.

Denise

I guess now I can get my introduction. I'm Denise Jackson. I'm 20 years old. I stood 5'3, weighing 148 pounds. Due to my Haitian roots, I had a coffee bean dark complexion. I loved myself and my skin. The two people that I didn't play about were Dinero and Kyra. They were all I had. As you know by now, Dinero is my brother. I've been the middleman for them two since we were kids. I have been praying for the day they stop playing and just be with each other already.

My love life was just now taking off so I couldn't be focused on them as much. I was dating Lanez; he was a dabbler. He dab in a little bit of this and that; whatever paid good. He was my chocolate boo. Me, I had a party planning business. I was well known around Nashville through De-signz Inc.

The party was coming to an end, and everyone was clearing out. Dinero and Kyng were carrying items to the car, loading them up and Kyra and I were packing things up.

"Where the fuck is Nitro ass at?" Kyra asked, looking around.

"Hell, if I know."

I grabbed some items that belong in the kitchen area and headed back to the kitchen. I walked in the kitchen, and I heard voices coming from the pantry area. I placed the items on the counter and walked over to the pantry and tried to make out the voices.

"What the fuck you mean you ain't get the abortion? Bitch, I gave you money to handle that." That sounded like Nitro.

"Because I thought about it, this is a gift from God," Tori said. *Oh my god,* I thought.

"You're tripping Tori; I ought to choke your ass right now," Nitro said.

"Oh, so now you gone whoop my ass like you be doing Kyra?" Tori said. I eased back knocking some pans off the counter.

"Fuck!" I said.

Tori and Nitro came out the pantry and saw me, and I was looking at them like a deer caught in headlights. I shook my head and ran out the kitchen.

Kyra

Sitting at a table, I was talking to Di'mond, Kyng's wife. He was business partners with Nitro and Dinero. We were laughing and talking about setting up play dates for the kids.

"Denise!" I heard Nitro voice boomed through the room. I looked up, and Denise was high tailing over towards me. Tori and Nitro were right behind her. Denise got to me and gave me this look.

"What's going on, NiNi?" I asked concerned.

Nitro stepped forward. "Don't listen to nothing she says, baby," he said. I looked back at Denise.

"What girl? You are scaring me," I said. Dinero and Kyng walked back in.

"What's up?" Dinero asked. Denise finally spoke. "I was in the kitchen putting some stuff up, and I heard voices coming from the pantry, so I went and took a listen. These two," she said, pointing to Nitro and Tori. "They were in deep conversation about him giving her abortion money, and her not getting the abortion," Denise said.

Everyone looked at Nitro and Tori.

"This bitch is lying," Nitro said.

"Aye, watch who you calling a bitch, my nigga," Dinero stepped up. Tori remained quiet.

"T, Tori. It was you the whole time. I knew I knew your voice from somewhere," I said. I stepped up and punched Tori in her shit. She fell back.

"Bitch, you going to jail!" she yelled.

"You think I give a fuck about going to jail. Both y'all motherfuckers around here creeping behind our backs the whole damn time!" I yelled. Tori stood up.

"Oh girl please, I know you been fucking Dinero. Just like I know you went to Memphis with him," Tori said. Nitro looked at me.

"What?" he asked. I nodded my head not even giving a fuck no more.

"Wait, so you been fucking this nigga behind my back and was pregnant the whole time but not by me?" Dinero asked Tori.

Tori laughed, and I charged after her again.

"He's been beating on Kyra too," Denise said, causing Dinero to look at me.

"He's been hitting on you, Ky?" Dinero asked me. "Is that what you were tryna cover up in the bathroom?" Dinero yelled at me, scaring me.

"Yes," I whispered. Dinero pulled his gun from his waistband and pointed it at Nitro.

"I suggest you use that bitch," Nitro said.

Kyng stepped out and grabbed Dinero arm pointing the gun towards the floor. "Look y'all need to chill this ain't the place for all that. I understand you're pissed off, but we don't make wild ass moves like this," Kyng said calmly as fuck. I heard little about Kyng and knew he was in some high-powered shit.

Dinero looked at Nitro. "This shit ain't over," he said, grabbing me by the hand and walking out the door. He hit the lock on his car and told me to get in. I did as I was told.

After a twenty-minute drive, we were in Brentwood. We pulled up to a home that I didn't recognize. "Whose house is this?" I asked Dinero.

"One of my other cribs I bought a couple of months ago. I know you ain't want to go back to where Tori had been staying." Dinero said. "You right about that," I said. We both stepped out of the car and headed inside.

I sat down on the couch and pulled out my phone to call my mom and check on Dinelle. Dinero came and sat on the couch beside me. I looked at him, and I could tell he was bothered by everything that had gone down.

"Penny for your thoughts?" I asked, placing my legs in his lap.

"A nigga just feels played right now. How I'm supposed to keep on working with this nigga after this? I can't do that shit, but I swear on everything I love he's gone see me and feel me," Dinero said.

I know I should've been like don't do anything, but Nitro deserved anything that came his way.

"So where does that put us?" I asked. Dinero looked at me in my eyes.

"Where we should've been a long damn time ago. Together," Dinero said, leaning over to kiss me.

I climbed on top of Dinero and placed my lips on his. Just feeling his tongue in my mouth cause the floodgates to open. I could feel the bulge in his pants and his breathing increase. He stood up and carried me to the bedroom. I laid on the bed staring at Dinero as he looked at me passionately. I bit my bottom lip and signaled for him with my finger. He removed his shirt and made his way over to me. I ran my hands down his chest, and he leaned down to plant kisses on my neck. I let out a soft moan and laid back on the bed. His hands found its way around my body as he removed my panties and flung them on the floor. He slowly traced my nipples with his tongue and eased down to my creamy center.

"Damn, I see she already wet," he said.

I giggled and closed my eyes as he placed his warm mouth on my pussy. Dinero's head game was on point. I moaned out in ecstasy, trying to keep calm. I arched my back because I was about to climax. Dinero had the tightest grip on my legs. I let out my juices in his mouth. Dinero lifted up and placed his body in between my legs. He entered me slowly and pulled back out as if he was trying to tease me. He entered me again, and this time he stayed planting his face in the crease of my neck.

"Damn Ky, why you so fucking wet?" he whispered in my ear. He picked up the pace.

Lifting himself up, he pushed my legs back by my head and was pumping harder. He was hitting my spot, and I felt I was about to cum again. I closed my eyes.

"Look at me," Dinero demanded. I quickly opened my eyes "This my pussy now?" he asked. I nodded my head, and he smacked my ass "I can't hear you, Ky," he said.

"Yes, it's yours," I said through a moan. His pace increase and he released in me. Dinero collapsed beside me, and we both got our breathing together.

"We ain't finished, I'm just taking a break," Dinero said. "This gone be an all-night thing," he said, cuddling up behind me and holding me in his arms.

I laughed and closed my eyes. It felt good being in the arms that I belonged in all alone.

Chapter 8

Nitro

It had been two months since all that shit went down between Dinero and I. The shit was now interfering with my money, so we most definitely had a problem. I was the least bit concerned about these bitches. Sitting in the barbershop getting my beard trimmed up and shit, my cell started to ring. I held up the phone and saw it was Kyng.

"Aye, hold up," I said, telling the barber and heading to the back to answer the phone. "Hello," I said.

"I really hate looking for people Nitro, that's not how you do business. I feel like you been dodging my calls," Kyng said calmly as fuck.

"Nah, I just felt there was no need to wrap anymore. Once I bring you this last stash of money, I will no longer be doing business with you," I told Kyng.

"So, you just now telling me this? Men don't do business like this. You never know when you might have to use me for business again. Since I know the situation, I'm gone let you slide on this bad business. Have me my money by tomorrow," Kyng said and hung up the phone.

"Jerk ass nigga," I said, heading back out to the barber chair to get my trim finished. I had some moves to make.

* * *

I headed out North to meet up with my homie Turk. It was time to hit Dinero where it hurts— in his motherfucking pockets. Pulling up to the trap, Turk and some of his homeboys were standing round kicking shit. I hopped out my ride and walked up to Turk.

“Look who came back to the Slums,” Turk said dapping me up. “Man, nigga I ain’t never left, but I need to holla at you on some real shit right quick,” I said. Turk nodded.

“Aite, come on,” he said, leading the way in the house. We stepped in the house, and Turk lit a blunt. I sat on the sofa across from him.

“So, what’s up?” Turk asked.

“I need some niggas that don’t mind going beast mode. I got a lick that will for sho put all y’all on the map,” I said.

“Who you tryna start beef with? Nigga you and Dinero been pushing weight like a motherfucker,” Turk asked.

“This ain’t got nothing to do with Dinero. I’m just finna start my own crew and get grimy. I got the first lick, but I need a team for the big one,” I said.

“I’m in if it doesn't involve Dinero cuz a nigga ain’t tryna get involved in nothing that pertains to Kyng and them St. Clair niggas,” Turk said.

“It’s not Dinero it’s another cat,” I lied. I needed a crew, and I knew Turk had a team of heavy hitters.

“Count me in then,” Turk said, giving me dap.

Kyra

While sitting at the computer looking at venues for a future client, my head started swarming. I had been working with Denise at De-signz so that I could do something instead of sitting on my ass. Dinero was trying to pull some strings so that I could at least go back to school. When I did that bid for Nitro, that charge didn’t look good on my record. I closed my eyes and rested my head in my hands. I heard Denise heels clicking on the floor.

“What’s wrong with you, Ky?” she asked. I lifted my head

“I have no clue. I feel like shit,” I said. I felt the contents in my stomach start to make its way up an I turned towards the wastebasket and let it go. “Ugh bitch, you could’ve gone to the bathroom. Denise said turning up her nose.

“I wasn’t gone make it,” I said. Denise was looking at me shaking her head.

“What?” I asked instantly getting aggravated.

“Somebody pregnant,” she said. I sat there quietly thinking when the last time I had a cycle was. I haven’t had a cycle since before Dinelle’s birthday.

"You don't look happy. I swear this seals the deal since you and my brother together now. Hell, all y'all need to do is get married," Denise said, rambling like always.

"I don't look happy because Denise most likely this is Nitro's baby and not Dinero's." I sighed, leaning back in my chair.

"Fuck," Denise said, which was my exact thought.

Denise

Leaving the shop to meet Lanez for lunch, I couldn't get out of there fast enough. Lanez did that me. He gave me butterflies. I unlocked my door and hopped in my Camaro to head to him. About ten minutes into my drive I looked up in the rearview, and it looked as if I was being followed. I decided to bust a quick right to see if they would do the same and they sure enough did. I continued to drive and called Lanez.

"Wassup, baby?" he answered.

"I think I'm being followed, but I'm about to pull up at the restaurant. Can you be outside?" I asked.

"Yeah, I got you," Lanez said.

I pulled up to the restaurant, parked, and got out. I walked over to Lanez, and we both turned to watch the black BMW stop. The window was tinted so darkly you couldn't even see in the car. Lanez put his hand on his pistol and started walking over to the car. As he neared the car, it sped off. Lanez looked back at me.

"You don't recognize the car?" Lanez yelled clearly pissed off. I shook my head no.

"I need a drink," I said my nerves were all over the place.

"Man, shawty, how can you think about drinking at a time like this? You don't know who them motherfuckers were," Lanez said.

"True but a bitch's nerves are on ten. I need to call my brother," I said.

"Nah, I'm your nigga, so I'll handle it. No need to run to your brother. That's what I'm here for." Lanez said, making me feel comfortable.

We walked into Redlands and had lunch, but in the back of my mind, I'm still thinking about who the fuck was following me.

Dinero

"Twenty, forty, sixty, eighty, a hundred," I said aloud, counting the last batch of the cash stacked up in front of me.

I placed the other half of the money in the duffle bag I had sitting on the table. I grabbed both bags and headed into the other room. Dropping the bags on the floor, I looked at my carrier.

"That's forty grand. Make sure you drop both those bags off at the address I'm about to give you. I know you got two stops, but I need you to follow exact orders. Drop those off first before you head to spot number two. Don't take them bags to the second spot," I demanded. I watched as he grabbed the bags

"Yo, that shipment of guns, I need to get a few out of there," I said buttoning up my suit jacket.

A nigga was dressed fresh as hell in my Tom Ford suit. I most definitely wasn't dressed to be in no damn trap house. I followed dude to the locked wall safe where we kept most of our guns. I grabbed two pieces out for Kyra and me.

Kyra

After leaving the office, I headed to the drug store to scoop me up a pregnancy test. When I got home, I was dreading this moment. The more I thought about it, I knew deep down inside I was indeed pregnant, and it belonged to Nitro. I swear I didn't want no dealings with his ass. I entered the home that Dinero and I now shared, heading upstairs to the bathroom. I threw my purse on the bed and went to the bathroom. I sat down on the toilet and removed the test from the wrapper. Holding the test still, I handled my business. I placed the cap back on the test and laid it on the sink. Washing my hands and looking at my reflection in the mirror, I shook my head because I had put on a few pounds.

"Sup?" I heard Dinero's deep voice from behind which caused me to jump. I placed my hand over the test and stood in front of it hopefully blocking his view.

"You scared me, bae," I said. Dinero looked edible in his suit he wore. He walked over and placed a kiss on my lips.

"I missed you," he said. I slid the test in my back pocket.

“I missed you too,” I said.

I felt Dinero hands roam down my back and were headed right towards my ass. *Fuck!* I thought. Dinero grabbed my ass and removed his face out of the crook of my neck. I felt him remove the test from my pants pocket.

“What the hell is this?” Dinero asked, holding the pregnancy test in my face. I nervously bit my lip.

“A pregnancy test,” I said. Dinero smirked.

“Well duh, clearly I see that. Why you tryna hide it is the question?” he said. I leaned back on the sink and placed my hands over my face.

“I’m not, I literally just took it. I don’t even know what it says,” I said. Dinero looked down at the test without saying anything, and a smile crept up on his face

“You’re pregnant,” he said. I felt all the color drain from my face. My heart felt like it crumbled into a million pieces. “Why don’t you look happy, Ky?” Dinero asked, lifting my chin.

“This baby is Nitro’s,” I said.

Dinero stepped back and looked at me with confusion or anger all on his face— I couldn’t tell. “You ain’t been with that nigga in months!” he yelled. I rolled my eyes because I refuse to believe Dinero was this damn stupid.

"Don't you think I know that. I was pregnant before Dinelle's party; I just didn't know!" I yelled.

"How you not gone know all this time?" he asked.

"Dinero, so much shit has been going on that I didn't notice any changes in my damn body," I said, walking away from him headed into the bedroom. I was pissed off now.

"Well, what you gone do? Cause Nitro's ass will be grass soon," Dinero said serious as all get out. My mouth flew open.

"Regardless how you feel about Nitro, this is still my child, Dinero. I don't like his ass either. Wait, what's your real issue with him besides what he did to me? You talking about killing this nigga over Tori? I sholl hope you ain't still bugging off that bitch," I asked.

"This ain't got nothing to do with Tori. He's disrespectful as fuck and needs to be handled," Dinero said.

"Well, I'm not getting rid of my baby because regardless of the bullshit he did, we were together and he took care of me," I said. Dinero sighed and threw his hands in the air.

"He took care of you, but where's your car at? Still at that nigga house, right? You ain't got shit to show clothes none of that. You need to schedule a doctor appointment so we can see exactly how far along you are," Dinero said.

Chapter 9

Tori

It was hot as fuck outside, and I was irritable as hell. I pulled my black BMW into my brother's apartment. I had been staying here after all that bullshit went down. I grabbed my purse and got out his car. Climbing the steps to his apartments, I ran into one of my brother's friend Turk.

"Damn, Tori. You need to stop playing with a nigga and let me take you out sometime," he said. I rolled my eyes. Turk was a grimy nigga, not my type. He had a little pocket change, but I could do bad by myself.

"Aite, I'm gone remember that. When a nigga come up though don't be out here clout chasing," he said. I turned around and flicked him a bird.

Using my key, I let myself in the house. "Sin!" I called out. Throwing my keys on the coffee table

"Sin Santiago!" I yelled again. I walked into the kitchen and grabbed a bottle of water.

"Bruh, stop calling my name like you a nigga's mama. I could have had a bitch in there with me," Sin said, walking into the kitchen.

"My bad nigga," I said.

"Why you got them little bitty ass shorts on?" he asked, turning up his face.

"Last I checked I was grown nigga damn," I said. Sin smacked his lips.

Sin looked just like our father. He had yella skin like me. He rocked that shaved sides and braids at the top look. Sin was tall as fuck at about 6'3. He played ball in school. He kept himself looking nice; he was all about his appearance.

"Where you been all day? Let me guess following them chicks around, huh?" he asked. I looked at him like he was crazy. He was right though; I spent my days and gas following around Kyra and Denise.

"Why are you wasting your time with that shit anyway?" he asked.

"Because of them, I lost my fucking child Sin. Them hoes gone pay for the pain they caused me!" I cried out. Sin curled his lips at me like he wasn't falling for my shit.

"They didn't cause you to lose your baby. That nigga Nitro beat the shit out of you. That nigga ain't shit!" Sin spat. "When this lick fall through, and I get this money, I'm gone give you your half, and you go back to New York with mama because you don't have no need to be here no more." Sin said. "I'll get up with you later," he said, kissing my forehead and heading out the door.

I sat back on the couch and took in what my brother said, but I was out for revenge. Them hoes running they mouth fucked up what I could've had. I loved my brother Sin, and what was even better nobody knew we were related except his close friend Turk. I was gone get even with everybody. I sure will be heading back to New York right after I put my plans in motion. These hoes were gone feel me.

Nitro

Weaving in and out of traffic, I bobbed my head to Meek Mills "Dreams and Nightmares". Tonight, was the night I started making Dinero's little world start to crumble. I made a right on Turk's block. I hopped out the rented Toyota Prius I copped. Every time I came over here, it was in something different. I couldn't have no witnesses that I had been linking up with a nigga like Turk. I walked up to Turk and dapped him up.

"What it do, nigga?" I asked.

"Shit, me and my niggas down to ride. I already went over everything with them. Shit should be easy as hell if it's like you claim," Turk said. I nodded.

"Can we take this inside?" I asked.

"Yeah, come on y'all," Turk said, and everyone turned to walk in the house.

"Yo, this my nigga Nitro I was telling y'all about. Nitro this my nigga Sin and my nigga Lanez," Turk introduced. I nodded at them. It was time to get to business.

"Ok so look, this nigga makes two drops to two different locations. I already watched the drops. They not gone pick up until midnight. So, we can get in and out both spots ten minutes top. At the first spot, we just need the cash. At the second spot grab the keys. That's what we need. After we get everything, I'll give y'all ya cut, and we can talk about starting up a team out here," I said quickly going over everything. Everyone nodded, and I could tell was eager to do this shit.

We hopped in Turk's beat up ass Crown Vic and headed to the first spot. "Now look Sin, when you go up to the door they gone let you in to serve you. Tell them you want a subway sandwich. They don't keep that shit bagged up, so he's gone go to the back. Look around and see if anybody else in there. Flick the porch light, signaling how many in there. That will be our cue; bout time you turn to walk out, we will be running in that bitch," I said, throwing out orders.

We pulled up at the spot.

"Park right here and cut the lights," I said. I looked at the cars outside, and it was the usual cats there. "Ok, most likely it's only two niggas in there. I recognize the car," I said.

"Man, how we know you ain't tryna set us up?" this nigga Lanez said. I turned around in my seat.

"The fuck you think you talking to, nigga? Don't you think you should've voiced your concerns before you hopped in the car with us?" I said pissed the fuck off.

"I'm just saying, this shit sounds too damn easy," Lanez said.

"Fuck all that you talking. Aite Sin, go head," I said. Sin nodded his head and got out the car. Dressed in all black, he ran across the street.

I watched as Sin walked up on the porch and knocked on the door. The door opened, and within seconds he was in. I looked at my watch and back at the door. The porch light blinked once "There it goes, let's go," I said, and we all hopped out the car, watching the area making sure it wasn't no witnesses out.

We walked in the yard and made our way up the steps no soon as my foot hit the top step, Sin was coming out the front door "Surprise nigga," I said, aiming my .357 magnum at Dinero's worker head. "Where the money at?" I asked.

"I don't know what you're talking about," dude said. Lanez reached behind him and removed the gun he had in his waistband. Turk came from the back room carrying a duffle bag.

"Well nigga, your services are no longer needed." *BANG!* I hit him dead in the head. "Let's go!" I yelled, and we all ran out the house and back to the car.

We hopped in the ride, and Turk peeled out. "Man, that shit was smooth as butter, I said, looking in the bag at the bills.

I laughed because a nigga didn't even need this money. This was just some shit just because Dinero thinks he can't get touched. The money I know he ain't gone miss, but once we get these keys, that nigga gone be sick.

We hit the block of the other spot, the main lick I was interested in. I signaled for Turk to cut the lights. "I know this nigga ain't gone have all his keys in one spot, he scatters them around, but I know for a fact it some in here with some cash too. We gone do the same shit we did at the other spot, but this time Lanez will go to the door," I spoke.

"Aite," Lanez said, exiting the vehicle. He walked up to the house and knocked on the door.

Watching my watch, this nigga was taking longer than expected. "What the fuck is taking this nigga so long?" I asked.

"Ion know nigga, but if my G don't send no signal in three minutes, I'm knocking off everything in that bitch," Turk said, pulling out his strap. The porch light finally went off three times.

"There it goes," I said. I reached under the seat and pulled out some extra artillery. Then exited the car. I pulled my ski mask down over my head, and Turk and Sin did the same. We stood on the side of the door and waited for Lanez to come out. The door opened, and we rushed in. "GET THE FUCK ON THE FLOOR" I yelled.

Two niggas got down. I signaled for Turk and Lanez to go look for the other nigga. I walked to the kitchen area and pulled out the makeshift hidden compartment we had, and it was two kilos in it sitting pretty. I grabbed the kilos and threw them in the duffle bag. Walking back in the living room, all three niggas was finally laying on the floor. *BANG! BANG! BANG*! I let off a shot each in the back of them niggas' heads. We ran back to the car and was out like a thief in the night.

"That nigga Dinero ain't gone know what hit him," I said, laughing out loud. Turk looked over at me.

"Dinero? Nigga, you said that it was some other niggas. I told you I wasn't finna get in no shit with them St. Clair niggas. You foul as fuck for that shit, G!" Turk yelled.

"Chill the fuck out, nigga. You either want this money and get put on or stay penny-pinching, my nigga," I said not really giving a fuck what he did. "Any of you niggas got a problem?" I asked.

"Nah nigga, just give me my shit," Lanez said.

Dinero

Stepping out of my office, I heard Kyra and Dinelle in the bathroom laughing and talking.

"Ma ma, luk," Dinelle said, pointing up at me. I smiled, and Kyra turned around and rolled her eyes and went back to bathing Dinelle. I shook my head at her attitude; she had a right to be mad. My phone buzzed, and I looked down at the screen.

"Yeah," I said.

"Nigga, we been hit!" my homie yelled through the phone. I walked away from the bathroom.

"What the fuck you mean we been hit?" I asked, starting to feel my blood boil.

"Cash and keys," was all he said.

"I'm on my way, meet me at shop," I said and ended the call. "Fuck!" I yelled.

I took off towards my bedroom. Walking into the closet, I removed the shirt and slacks I had on. I grabbed a pair of black Nike joggers and slid them on. I threw on a black t-shirt and pulled the matching Nike jacket off the hanger and threw that on. I removed all my jewelry. I turned to my shoe side of the closet and grabbed a pair of Nike Air Max.

"What's going on, and why you got on all that hot ass shit?" Kyra asked. I turned around and faced her.

"Baby, somebody done hit two of my spots. The crazy thing I know exactly who the fuck it is. This is why I said that nigga whose baby you're carrying got to motherfucking go!" I yelled.

I know part of what I said may seem fucked up, but a nigga was heated at the moment. If she couldn't see why Nitro's ass needed to be handled, Kyra and I were going to have serious problems. Kyra stood there with her mouth open. I knew she wanted to say something, but she didn't. I stepped from around her and headed to my office. I felt her on my heels. I headed over to the safe and removed my gun. I turned to Kyra. She looked so innocent; her thick curls were all over the place. She leaned against the door with her arms crossed. I walked over to her and gently grabbed her arms.

"Look, Ky. A nigga is sorry. I swear its so much shit going through my head right now. I find myself asking will we ever just get to that place where we're stress-free and happy. Look how far we come. We gone get it right, you gone be my rider and eventually my wife. This nigga Nitro's got to die," I said, leaning in and kissing her. I felt the tears running down her face. "I'll be back. I love you," I said.

"I love you too," Kyra whispered.

Chapter 10

Dínero

The shop was a clothing spot that I was about to open soon and give to Kyra to run. I sat in my office listening to my nigga David.

“Man, it was more than one nigga with him though. Shit was smooth as hell,” David said. I had lost four workers.

“Make sure to tell their families the funeral expenses are taken care of,” I said. Security popped his head in.

“Boss, it’s some cats out here said they need to talk to you it’s important,” he said.

I looked at David, and he shrugged his shoulders. I made sure I had my hand on the trigger, and David had his ready also. “Send them in,” I said.

Security opened the door to let them in, in walked two niggas I knew one, this nigga Lanez was my sister boyfriend. The other nigga, I wasn’t familiar with.

“What you doing here, Lanez?” I asked. The other nigga spoke first

“I felt we needed to come to you and let you know the deal on them hits you just took. I’m Turk by the way,” Turk said. I sat up in my chair

“And what you niggas know about my shit getting hit?” I said ready to lay these niggas out where they stood.

“Calm down, homie, I’m not here on no fuck shit. I’m here to fix it. We hit your spots,” Turk said. I stood up and pointed my gun at Turk's head, and David pointed his at Lanez.

“Wait mane; it ain’t like that. Hear a nigga out,” Lanez said, Turk started speaking again.

“That nigga Nitro came to me on some get rich quick shit, so a nigga was down. But off the wam I asked that nigga if this shit had any connection to you because I know who you run with and a nigga ain’t want no beef with no cartel niggas. That nigga flat out lied talking bout nah this ain’t Dinero shit. So, shit, I told my crew, and we went ahead with that nigga. It wasn’t until we left the second spot, I guess he got too excited and let that shit slip mentioning your name. I confronted that nigga, but he was like take the money or don’t. We both got the cut he gave us and was bringing it to you,” Turk said.

I put my gun down, sticking it back in my waist. I had taken in all this nigga said. I sat down at my desk. David still had his gun pointed at Lanez.

“Put ya gun up, nigga,” I said. I looked at Turk. “How many of y’all was it?” I asked.

“Just me, Lanez, Nitro, and my nigga Sin,” he answered.

"Where this nigga Sin at?" I asked. Turk and Lanez looked at each other, and I looked at them. "Get to talking nigga; you been talking fine up until now!" I yelled. I was getting aggravated.

"We told that nigga we were coming to see you, he took his cut and bounced," Turk said.

I sighed and leaned back in my chair resting my hands on top of my head. "You niggas talk too much. You do know your homie done went and told this nigga what the hell it is y'all did?" I said laughing.

"Give me my cash," I demanded. They placed the money on the desk. "I appreciate y'all coming to me and keeping it real. I know y'all seen it as a quick come up. Right now, I could use both of you niggas. Since y'all done killed my fucking workers, I need new workers at them spots. In the meantime, tell you nigga Sin about another lick that's gone be bigger than that and get him to get that nigga Nitro in on it. This is gone be the biggest dummy hit," I said, laughing at my plan I was thinking about.

"Dummy hit?" Turk asked.

"Counterfeit bills and fake kilos. This nigga thinks he finna flip my product on the street, which he will after what he just got, but this next one he's gone lose all his fucking customers. I still got some kinks to work out so play shit cool like I said and put that bird in Sin ear," I said, dismissing them. If this nigga wanted to play, we could play.

Kyra

The time had come for me to head to the doctor to confirm what I already knew, but Dinero insisted that I go anyways because it was a little chance the baby could be he his, so he thought. Dinero switched lanes through traffic, nodding his head to the music.

"Aye look," he said, turning the music down. I turned my head facing him. "It's a lot of shit been going down lately, and shit might get hectic. I need you to be able to hold your own in case you find yourself in a fucked up predicament. Not saying shit to scare you or not even saying that something may happen, but I want my woman to be prepared. When we leave the doctor's office, I'm taking you to meet my partner; he owns a skilled training gun range," Dinero said. "Niggas like to fuck with anything a nigga loves when they can't get to who they want," Dinero said.

I knew shit was getting crazy in the streets. Dinero was spending less time at home over the past couple of days.

"I'm down," I said. Dinero grabbed my hand, giving me a squeeze.

Shortly after we pulled up at the doctor's office, Dinero stepped out and made his way around the vehicle and opened my door.

"Thank you, baby," I said. It was hot and humid outside and instantly I got irritated.

"Stop frowning Ky; you're looking too fine for that shit," Dinero said.

It was hot as hell, but I felt myself blushing. I was looking cute in my Gucci floral print sundress and sandals that Dinero had copped for me. We were laughing and walking across the street when out of nowhere a Black BMW came flying down the street. Thanks to another person who were following behind us yelling out "Look out!" we were able to step back in time enough.

"What the fuck?" Dinero said as we watched the car turn the corner quickly.

"Oh my god, are you guys ok?" the woman behind us asked.

"Yes, thank God," I said. I was ok, but Dinero had that look of a murderer in his eyes.

"That maniac was driving too fast down this street," the woman said, walking off shaking her head. I looked at Dinero.

"Baby, what the fuck? Do you have any idea who that was?" I asked. Dinero shook his head and grabbed my hand as we tried crossing the street again for the second time.

"This is why I need to get you to the range ASAP; that could have been anybody. That's bitch shit tho," Dinero said, looking puzzled. We headed on into the building to my appointment.

Sitting on top of the table in the room, it was eerily quiet. The doctor had just confirmed that I was twelve weeks. I knew it already, but I wondered what was going through Dinero's head. We both sat there.

"Say something Dinero. The silence is killing me," I whispered. He had this look of defeat on his face.

"I mean it is what it is. Yeah, a nigga would've loved for that to be my kid you are carrying, seeing that I missed that opportunity with Dinelle. I understand that's your child also and I know we all was playing around. Plus, I know deep down inside if you could change things you would. I'm here for you. I'm that baby's pappi," he said.

We both busted out laughing, and I threw my arms around him and kissed him with so much passion. We walked out of the doctor's office, and Dinero was all in his phone.

"Come on we got to get to the range. I'm gone drop you off for a little bit because I got to handle something, but I'll be right back. It's a change of clothes in the trunk because you need to be comfortable," Dinero said.

"Ok baby," I said.

I placed my hand on my flat tummy and thought about how in January I will be a mommy of two. It was so much I wanted to do, but things will have to be put on hold once again. Looking out the window, we pulled up to a secluded gun range. Dinero got out and popped the trunk as I got out of the passenger side. I waited by the side of the car as he carried the bag over to me.

“Come on,” he said, and we walked into the building. The smell of gunpowder filled the air.

“What it do, Trev?” Dinero said, dapping his homie up. Trev was a military army brat. He knew everything it was to know about guns and his sniper skills was A1.

“Baby, this my white boy, Trev.” Dinero turned to me introducing me.

“Hey,” I said, holding my hand out for him to shake. “Where’s the bathroom? I’m gone go change,” I asked Dinero. Dinero pointed his hand.

“Down the hall on the right. I’m gone be right back after I finish taking care of what I need to handle,” Dinero said, kissing me on my cheek. I kissed him back and headed to get changed.

I had changed into some leggings and a t-shirt and pulled my hair up into a messy bun. The bathroom door opened and in walked a chippy white chick.

“Hi, I’m Bianca; Trev’s wife. He sent me in here to see if you're all ready to get started,” she said.

“Oh, yeah. Let’s go,” I said.

“Well come on, honey,” she said. I don’t know where she was from, but she was country as hell. “You can put your things in here, and I’ll lock the office up,” Bianca said. I laid my items in a chair and Bianca locked the room door.

"So, I heard congrats where in order on the little bundle of joy," Bianca said, catching me off guard. I gave her a confused look. "Oh, Dinero told Trev to take it easy on you because you were expecting," Bianca said.

I saw this fine ass nigga walking towards me I should be ashamed for giving him the look I was giving him.

"Thank you," I said to Bianca, realizing I never responded to her. The guy stood in the stall next to us smiling at me before he disappeared.

"Is this you guys first child?" Bianca asked.

"No, we have a daughter together, this is actually my ex's child. Long story," I said.

"No need to go into details," she said.

"Alright Sin, you can head over to the course outside," Trev said, walking over to the fine guy I was eye stalking earlier. He made his way over to me

"You ready? Bout time I'm done with you, you'll be able to shoot at anything moving," Trev said.

Nitro

I was sitting over at Ivyanna's one of the many bitches I was messing with to keep my mind off Kyra. She was a bad little stripper bitch I had been knocking down. She came in the living room and handed me a blunt she rolled. I took a hit and leaned my head back on the couch. My cellphone rang. I grabbed it off the table and saw it was Sin. Sin turned out to be a decent cat. He had told me Lanez and Turk were going to Dinero, but I guess they had a change of plans because they had kept the money and was coming up on another lick soon.

"Hello," I said, hitting the blunt.

"You at Ivy's crib? I need to stop by and holla at you," Sin said.

"Yeah come through," I said, disconnecting the call.

About five minutes later, Sin came walking through the door. "Wassup nigga?" Sin said, dapping me up.

"Not shit; just got done counting up this money from the last pick up," I said.

"So, what's up, what you need to holla at me about?" I asked. Sin looked at Ivy and looked at me like he wanted her to leave.

"Can't you see a nigga is tryna have a conversation," I said to Ivy. She rolled her eyed and left the room.

"Check this out ain't old girl you use to mess with name Kyra?" Sin asked, causing me to sit up.

"Yeah, why you ask?" I asked.

"I was at white boy Trev's today, and I saw Dinero, that's what caught my attention. Then I saw shorty come in with him. I was in the stall next to her and overheard her telling Bianca that the baby she was carrying wasn't his but her ex's," Sin said, catching me all the way off guard.

"You sure this what you heard?" I asked.

Sin nodded his head yeah. Damn a nigga about to be a daddy. I got to try and get my bitch back. I'll be damn if Dinero plays daddy to mines.

"You heard anything else about the lick?" I asked Sin.

"Not yet, they said they would keep me posted. You know I got you," Sin said.

"That's what's up nigga. I'm gone get up with you later," I said. Sin got up and headed out.

"Ivyanna!" I yelled. Ivy's thick ass came walking in the living room.

"Yeah what's up?" she said with a slight attitude. "You can drop the attitude. You remember what we talked about?" I asked. She smiled.

"Hell yeah," she answered a little bit too happy.

"Set that shit up, and if he comes in there make your money," I said.

Ivy walked off to get ready for work. I had so many ways I could bring Dinero down and one thing I knew for sure. Dinero couldn't function without Kyra. Hell, I couldn't function without her.

Chapter 11

Kyra

It had been two whole months since I started training with Trev. You can call it somewhat of an addiction now. I loved the way the steel felt in my hand. It gave me a sense of power. Dinero thought it was funny how I spent a lot of my time there. If I wasn't helping Denise at her office, I was at Trev's. I had mastered the perfect hit of targets, everything there was to know about a gun, and how to shoot it. I was finishing up when Bianca came in.

"Hey girl, here again I see," she said. I laughed.

"You sound like your husband and Dinero. I'm gone take a break after today. It's time for me to start getting prepared for this big head boy I'm having," I said.

"Oh my god, you're having a boy? When did you find out?" she asked.

"We went yesterday," I said. I grabbed my bag and kissed Bianca on the cheek and told Trev bye.

Walking to my car, I called Dinero to see where he was at. After six rings, he didn't answer so I hung up. I reached into my bag and grabbed my keys so I could unlock the door, and the keys hit the ground. I bent over to pick my keys up.

"I sholl miss hitting that fat ass from the back," I heard coming from someone I sholl didn't want to see. I stood up and saw his reflection in the tint of my car window.

"I was told I could find you here. I heard you live in this bitch." Nitro said.

I kept my back towards him and moved my bag in front of my growing belly before turning around. *Damn, he looked good.* What the fuck? This baby was fuckin' my hormones up because I can't believe I even thought that. Nitro took a step towards me, and I stepped back.

"Why you tryna cover your belly, I know you pregnant with my seed, bruh," Nitro said, moving the bag out the way.

He reached out about to touch my stomach, and I smacked his hand away. He chuckled a menacing laugh. "So, I can't touch your stomach Kyra?" he asked.

"Nitro, what the fuck you want?" I asked. "Damn for real, this where we at now? You carrying my damn child and I gotta hear that shit from somebody other than you? You good at doing that shit ain't cha? You did Dinero that same way and now you are trying to keep me from my kid," Nitro said. I sighed.

I turned around and unlocked the door opening so that I can get in.

"Kyra, please can I touch your stomach? I just want to see about my kid," Nitro said. I knew at that moment I needed to leave, but I couldn't.

"Come on," I said. Nitro stepped closer and placed his hand on my stomach and why in the hell my son kicked.

“What was that?” Nitro asked with widened eyes.

“He kicked,” I said.

“He?” Nitro asked. Fuck, I didn’t mean to say that. I nodded my head yeah. “Man Kyra, you are carrying my son, and you were really gone make me miss out on all of that,” he said. Why in the fuck was I feeling bad?

“Nitro, real shit you and Dinero got too much shit going on, that’s why? Plus, you put your hands on me a little too much. I lost all respect for you,” I said. “Look I got to go,” I told Nitro trying to close my door he finally let go of the door. “This not the last time you gone see me and don’t think you gone keep me from my son!” Nitro yelled as I pulled away.

My nerves were all over the place after seeing Nitro. If Dinero found about that shit, he would cut me off for a motherfucking fact. I had worked up an appetite.

“Call Denise,” I said to the car Bluetooth. The phone rang, and Denise answered.

“Hey girl!” she said.

“Bitch, I’m hungry,” I said. Denise laughed “Tell me something I don’t know. Come scoop me,” Denise said.

“Aite, I’ll be there in ten minutes,” I said. I called Dinero again.

“Wassup, Ky?” he answered.

“Why you ain’t answer when I called earlier?” I asked.

“Damn, a nigga was in the shower, I had to get ready for this meeting tonight,” Dinero said.

“Yeah, okay. Don’t get beat up, nigga,” I said.

“I want you to beat me up. Hell, you’ve been stingy with the pussy lately,” Dinero said.

“Shut up boy, I might be in the mood tonight when you get home,” I said. “I’m just letting you know I’m about to meet up with your sister to get something to eat then I’ll pick Dinelle up from daycare,” I said.

“Aite then baby,” he said. “I love you.”

“I love you too, Ky,” he said, and we ended the call.

I pulled up at Denise house and texted her letting her know I was outside. I let down the visor in the car and pulled my hair out of the ponytail I had it in. I wanted to cut my shit so bad. I ran my fingers through it to loosen my curls. I applied a little of Yves Saint Laurent gloss to my lips and put my earrings back in. Denise came walking out to the car, and I busted out laughing when she opened the door.

“Bitch, I see Lanez got a hold of that ass. You ought to be ashamed walking out here like that,” I said messing with her.

“Fuck you, Kyra. But girl yes, he always be trying to get it in before he leaves the fucking house. Bitch my pussy can’t take no more beatings,” she said. We both fell out laughing.

“Girl, where you want to eat at?” I asked Denise. She shook her head and looked at me.

“You the pregnant one, I’m not fin to get cussed out because you want one thing and not what I want,” Denise said. “I do want some Chimichangas,” I said. “Well go to Las Maracas so that I can get a margarita, Denise said. I put the car in drive and headed to East Nashville.

I was going back and forth with myself debating if I should tell Denise about my run-in with Nitro. I knew how she felt about him and if I told her she most likely would tell Lanez if not Dinero. I’ll just keep my mouth shut for now.

Dinero

Shit was looking good. Kyng came through with the fake kilos and counterfeit bills. I was gone set that shit up ASAP. I had to meet with one of Kyng’s friends in a few to check out the goods. I stood in the mirror and brushed my waves. Making sure I was on point, I gave myself a once over, and I was ready. I checked my watch to make sure I would be on time. I had a little time to spare, so I headed to the closet and changed shirts. Looking for a shirt to throw on. I grabbed a Balmain white t-shirt to go with the jeans I had on. I put on a pair of Gucci Frames and headed out the door. Tonight, I decided to take my black on black Mercedes G-Wagon. I hit the locks and hopped in my shit and peeled out.

I found myself nodding my head to some damn SZA "The Weekend". I shook my head at the song and knew Kyra's ass been in here listening to this shit; she was the last person in here. I didn't bother changing it. About twenty minutes later, I arrived at the strip club. I sat in the car and called David.

"Aye yo bruh, where you at? Aite I'm in the parking lot," I said and hung up the phone.

I saw David pulling in, and I flashed my lights so he could see where I parked. David parked his truck beside mines and hopped out. I walked over to where he stood.

"Man, you sure you want to go in here?" David asked. I looked at him like he was crazy. "Man, we just gone go in here and check this shit out, maybe have a drink or two and vamp," I said.

"I ain't never been to no strip club in the daytime with this many cars in the parking lot," David said, looking around. I laughed.

"Man, come on," I said as we walked inside.

When we got inside in the club, I headed to a booth and sat down. This bad ass chick walked over. "Welcome to Fantasy. Can I help you gentlemen?" the girl asked.

I squinted my eyes because shorty looked mad familiar, I was trying to remember where I remember shorty from, that's when it hit me. Freshman year of high school we went out for about three months. Kyra would shit a motherfucking brick right now if she knew about this.

“Ivyanna?” I asked.

“In the flesh.” She said. She gazed at me for a few minutes.

“Dinero Jackson!” she yelled.

I stood up, and she damn near jumped in my arms. Ivyanna was a cool ass chick. The last I heard from her she had got in some trouble and moved away.

“Damn, I ain’t seen you since high school,” I said.

“I know right, I been back for about a year working right here,” she said.

“That’s what’s up, can you tell your boss that I’m here. He is expecting me,” I said.

“Sure, we gone have to catch up when you finish,” she said.

I nodded my head and watched her twist off. I adjusted my dick in my pants because she had me on brick right about now. I looked at David, and all he did was shake his head.

“What nigga?” I asked.

“She looks like trouble; Kyra’s gone snatch both y’all asses,” David said. Ivy came walking back over to our table.

“He said to give him about ten minutes but to get started on this bottle,” she said, placing a bucket with D’usse in it on the table.

“Preciate it,” I said. Ivy winked and walked off.

Sipping on my second glass of D'usse. Cardo finally showed his face. "What's up Dinero, I'm sorry about the wait I had some loose ends to tie up about some paper," he said, apologizing.

"It's all good," I said.

"Y'all bring that bottle and let's take this back in my office so we can get down to business, I think I kept you guys waiting long enough," he said.

I grabbed the bucket and followed Cardo back to his office. We walked down a long dark hall and entered a room that was laid the fuck out. This shit looked like a sex dungeon slash pimp chambers.

"Have a seat," Cardo said. "Take a look at this."

Cardo snapped his fingers, and a Puerto Rican chick came out carrying two suitcases placing them on the table in front of us. Cardo leaned forward and opened the suitcases. One was filled with money and the other kilos of coke. I leaned forward and picked up a couple of pieces of money and examined them.

"This shit looks real as fuck," I said, handing the bills to David. Cardo smiled in agreement. He handed me a knife so that I could cut the package open.

"My Mexican homies made that shit. You can cook it up and all that, but it's nothing. No high," Cardo said.

"My nigga, this all looks good enough for what I'm trying to do. What I owe you?" I asked.

“Any job for Kyng is free with me. You just know where to come if you ever need me again,” Cardo said.

“That’s what’s up,” I said.

“Let’s finish off this damn bottle,” Cardo said.

* * *

Two hours later, I was still at the strip club. “Man Cardo, a nigga’s got to go, I done been here too damn long,” I said.

“Aite, it was nice doing business with you. You’re welcome here anytime, bro,” Cardo said. I shook his hand.

“Thanks for the hospitality,” I said.

Cardo shook David's hand, and we both exited his office heading back down the hall. Halfway down the hall, I felt someone grab my hand I looked up, and it was Ivy with this seductive ass look on her face. She was pulling me towards a room David turned around and looked at me.

“Bruh,” he said.

“I’ll be back,” I said. I followed Ivy into the room, and she closed and locked the door behind her.

“Dinero, seeing you done something to me. I can’t control myself,” she said, pushing me back on the couch. *Oh, hell nah,* I thought. *What the fuck was I doing*? The liquor had me wanting to bend Ivy ass over this couch and give her the business, but my mind was telling me to get the fuck out of there.

"Nah, I got a girl, Ivy. I can't do this," I said. She sat down on top of me.

"Somebody wants to stay even if you don't," she said, talking about my dick because he was on brick once again. I closed my eyes, and she grabbed my face. I felt her tongue slide into my mouth. I didn't want to kiss her back. *Fuck it*. I kissed her back. She stood up and parted my legs undoing my pants. My mans was standing at attention when she let it out of its cage.

"Ummmm," she said.

She dropped to her knees and took all of me in her mouth. I grabbed the back of her head and closed my eyes as she did her thing on the mic. I was trying to compose myself because it had been a minute since I had some pussy. Ivy stopped, and I grabbed her and placed her on the couch.

"Bend over," I said.

She did exactly what she was told except she said fuck the couch and bent over and grabbed her ankles. I entered her from behind. "Shit girl, your pussy tight as fuck," I said.

I started stroking and got my rhythm going. My phone started ringing. I kept my stroke going and looked at the phone it was Denise. I placed the phone back in my pocket and kept hitting Ivy from the back. She was throwing that shit back like a pro. My phone rang again, but I didn't even bother looking at it, I felt myself about to nut, and my phone rang again.

"Fuck!" I yelled, shooting off inside of Ivy. I was pissed the fuck off because motherfuckers kept calling my damn phone. I grabbed my phone.

"What man, damn?" I yelled in the phone.

"Dinero, Kyra's been shot!" Denise yelled in the phone. "Where y'all at?' I yelled, trying to pull my damn pants up.

"Vanderbilt," she said.

"I'm on my way," I said, hanging up the phone.

"Is everything ok?" Ivy asked. Hell, I forgot about her ass that quick.

"Nah man, in here trying to catch a fucking nut that I had no business catching my girl been shot and she pregnant," I said, leaving Ivy on the couch and running out the room.

Ivy stood up and got herself together, walking over to the phone. She had recording the whole thing.

Nitro: Here's your fucking video and btw yo baby mama's been shot.

Chapter 12

Kyra

Walking out of Las Maracas, Denise and I were walking back to my car when a Black BMW pulled up beside us. "That's the car that was following me awhile back," Denise said.

I turned and looked and the window let down. I reached in my bag. "Stupid ass bitch!" Tori yelled, letting off several shots.

Denise and I took off running. Once the shots stopped, and Tori had pulled off, I heard Denise yelling, "Kyra, you ok?" She came running over to me.

"I'm good," I said. I touched my stomach making sure my baby was ok.

"Kyra, you have blood coming from your pants and shirt!" Denise yelled. "Oh my god." She started panicking grabbing her phone. I looked down and saw the blood, I guess I didn't feel it because my adrenaline was rushing, but when I saw the blood, I passed out.

Dinero

A nigga did a hundred all the way to Vandy. "Fuck!" I yelled, hitting the steering wheel.

I looked in the rearview and David was trailing me. I pulled up at the front and hopped out "Sir you can't park here!" I heard somebody yell

"David take care of that!!" I yelled, running into the hospital. I called Denise asking where they were at. She gave me the room number, and I ran all the way there. I walked into the room, and Denise ran over to hug me.

"Is she ok?" I asked.

"Yeah, she was hit twice once in the arm which went clean through and once in the leg, but that was just a graze," Denise said.

"Is the baby ok?" I asked.

"Yeah, there still monitoring it just to be safe. Where the hell were you? I was blowing up your phone." Denise asked. I ignored her question

"How the fuck did this happen?" I asked.

"We were leaving the restaurant, and this black BMW pulled up…"

"A black BMW, that same car was trying to run over Kyra and me at the doctor office," I said, interrupting Denise.

"Well, it was following me one day, and Lanez ran up on it, and it pulled off. It's that bitch Tori. She rolled the window down and said some shit before she started shooting. Crazy ass bitch, wait to I see her ass," Denise said.

"Nah wait till I catch that bitch, them classes gone pay off because I'm gone murk that bitch," Kyra spoke startling Denise and me.

I rushed over to the bed and leaned in and kissed Kyra. Kyra moved her head. "Ugh you stink, you been drinking?" she asked.

"Um yeah, I had a few drinks," I said. I hope that was all she could smell.

Kyra

Dinero smelled of alcohol and Victoria's Secret Crush perfume. I knew I wasn't fucking tripping. I looked at Dinero, and I noticed what looked like makeup or lipstick on the bottom of his shirt.

"Come here, baby," I said. Dinero walked over to me. I lifted his shirt and instantly got sick at the sight of the dried up cum stains at the top of his black ass boxers. I flicked his shirt down and rolled my eyes.

"Who was she?" I whispered. Dinero looked confused and leaned closer to me

"What you say, baby?" he asked. *SMACK!*

"I said who the fuck was she?" I yelled. Denise walked over to the bed

"What the fuck Kyra, what's going on?" she asked. David walked into the room.

"Why don't you ask your brother about them nasty ass nut stains on his boxers and why his fucking shirt got all this damn makeup on it right here," I said showing them and Dinero the shit I was seeing. Dinero looked down and shook his head

"Baby, it's not what you think?" Dinero said.

"Don't insult me right now Dinero. So, whatever lie you think you about to tell me, I don't want to hear shit but the truth," I said.

I was hurting. I wanted to cry so bad, but I wasn't about to let it show. Dinero sighed. "Can y'all give us a minute?" Dinero asked Denise and David.

"Nope, they stay right here. I'm sure David ass already know what the fuck you did, so I'm all motherfucking ears." I said.

"Aite, I went to the strip club and ran into an old friend. During the business meeting, we had a couple of bottles a nigga was drunk. She came on to a nigga hard, and I fucked her," Dinero said.

"You fucking nasty ass strippers now?" I asked.

"Who was she?" I asked.

"Ivyanna," Dinero said. I looked at Denise, and she looked at me, and we both looked at Dinero. "Yo ex-bitch from school?" Denise asked.

"Wow, so while Denise was blowing your phone up and you kept ignoring her calls it was because you were knee deep in some pussy?" I asked. Dinero looked defeated.

"Look, man, I'm sorry," Dinero said.

"Get out," I said.

"What, I'm not going nowhere," Dinero said.

"GET OUTTTTT!" I yelled.

The tears were falling so hard my eyes were burning. Dinero and David headed out the room. Dinero looked back at me, and I turned my head while Denise consoled me. My phone buzzed, and I looked down it was a number I didn't know. I opened the message, and it was a video of Dinero fucking Ivyanna. Denise took my phone and just continued to hold me.

Nitro

When Ivy sent me that text, I wasn't really worried about the video. The bottom part was what caught my attention. I called Ivy.

"Yo, what was that shit about my baby mama being shot," I asked.

"All I know is he got a call he started panicking, and he said his gal got shot and she was pregnant. He left out," Ivy said.

"Did you hear what hospital she was at?" I asked. "I think the girl said Vanderbilt," Ivy said.

"Aite," I said hanging up.

* * *

I sat in the parking lot waiting until I saw Dinero get in his car and pull off. I hopped out my car, pulling my hat down over my eyes. I made it into the hospital unnoticed. I walked up to the front desk.

"Can I help you?" the nurse asked.

"Yeah, the mother of my child was brought here, her name is Kyra Mitchell. I think they said she had been shot," I said. The nurse type a few things in her computer.

"Ok, yes she's in room 426," she said.

"Thank you," I said, heading to her room. I didn't know if she was gone trip out or not, but I wanted to know if my son was ok. I made it to the room and knocked on the door.

"Come in," I heard her say. I opened the door and stepped in the room. No one was there but Denise and her.

"What are you doing here?" Denise asked. I looked at her and rolled my eyes. "I heard what happen, is the baby ok?" I asked.

"How you know what happened?" Denise asked.

"Yo bitch the one who did this," Denise said.

"What you mean my bitch, who Tori?" I asked. I looked at Kyra she nodded her head yes.

"I ain't seen Tori since I kicked her ass out. But now when I see that hoe, she gone make me fuck her up," I said. I walked closer to the bed and placed my hand over Kyra's stomach. "Hey lil' man, can you move for daddy for me like you did last time?" I asked.

"Last time, what the fuck is going on, Kyra?" Denise asked.

"Nothing, Denise chill out," Kyra said.

"You know what you and my brother and all these damn games y'all playing is pissing me off. Then you up here fraternizing with the enemy like everything kosher. You better pray my brother doesn't find out," Denise said, storming out the room.

"Nitro, don't think nothing is gone come out of this. I'm still with Dinero, but I appreciate you coming and checking on me and your son.

Fuck! I can't mention the video to her because she will know I had something to do with it.

Dinero

I couldn't believe the shit that just went down. A nigga was fucking up in a major ass way. I'm hoping and praying Kyra doesn't leave me over this. I was back at the crib chilling with David. I sat with my head resting in my hands.

"I know you don't want to hear this shit right now, but I told you something was off with old girl," David said. I looked up.

"You right, I don't want to hear that," I said, picking up the phone to call my sister.

"Hello," I heard Denise voice.

"Hey, how is Kyra?" I asked. "When I left she was just fine," Denise said.

"Damn man, a nigga fucked up big time, huh?" I asked Denise. Denise huffed.

"I mean you fucked up, both y'all got issues. You know somebody sent her video to her phone," Denise said. I looked at David.

"A video? Of what?" I asked. "Nigga a video of you fucking Ivy. You didn't look to be drunk as you claim. You seem to be enjoying it," Denise said.

"That bitch set me up! I bet Nitro's ass had something to do with it!" I yelled.

"Yeah, I bet he did too, tryna make his way back to his baby mama. You know Nitro's knows about the baby?" Denise said. My face was screwed up.

"How the fuck he know about the baby?" I asked.

"I'm not about to get into all that but know he knows," Denise said. I was getting pissed by the minute.

"Why in the fuck would you bring the shit up and not speak on it?" I asked.

"Oh my god, y'all getting on my damn nerves. Kyra told him!" she screamed and hung up the phone in my face. I looked at the phone like I know this bitch didn't hang up on me. I looked at David.

"Denise just told me it's a video and that Kyra told Nitro about the baby," I said. David shook his head.

"Man, y'all got some *Love & Hip Hop* shit going on around this bitch," David said.

"I can't believe Kyra," I said.

Chapter 13

Tori

I'm packing up my bags so that I could leave this damn place. My job was almost done. I had one more thing to do, and then I was out of here. I don't know if Kyra got hit or not, but I pray that bitch and her baby died. Sin had given me the money I needed to leave town, thanks to that lick he hit with Nitro. Nitro was so damn dumb at times. He needed to be aware of the people he had working for him. I laughed at the thought of how he just got played.

I walked towards Sin room and knocked on the door. "Yeah!" he yelled out.

"Open the door," I said. I heard Sin scrambling around, and the door opened

"What?" he asked.

"I'm ready," I said.

"Man, sis, I ain't feeling that shit; you gone have to do that shit yourself. I'm not about to put my hands on you. What is your point in all this? Please just take the money and go to New York before something happens to you," Sin pleaded to me. All that shit fell on deaf ears.

"You know what Sin fuck it, I'll do it myself," I said, turning around heading to my bedroom. I pulled out my phone and called my home girl Kesha.

"Hey girl, you want to make some quick cash?" I asked her.

"Hell yeah," she said.

"Cool, I'm heading to you right now," I said. I grabbed my purse and my suitcase and headed out the door. Unlocking my BMW, I threw the bags in the car and drove off.

I pulled up at Kesha's. I hated coming over here; she lived in University Court housing projects. All the tricking she be doing, and she couldn't buy decent housing. I hopped out and made sure I locked my doors and walked to Kesha's house. When I finally got to her apartment. I knocked on the door, and she came to it.

"Hey boo," she said, opening the door to let me in.

"Hey girl," I said. "What you been up to? I ain't heard from you in a minute," Kesha asked.

"Girl nothing tying up loose ends before I head back home. That's what I need your help with," I said.

"Shit, I'm down. I can always use some extra cash," Kesha said.

"Cool. "I need you to punch me a couple of times," I said. Kesha's mouth flew open, and she twisted her face up.

"Bitch, what kind of shit you on?" she asked me. I rolled my eyes.

"Bitch, do you want this $500 or not?" I asked, showing irritation.

Kesha drew back and punched my ass so fast that I didn't see that shit coming at all. She hit me two more times in my face. Blood flew from my lip. I touched my lip and smiled.

"Grab my arms and shit," I demanded. Kesha grabbed my arms and threw me on the couch and kept planting punches on me "Ok bitch, damn that's enough!" I yelled.

Kesha must've had some pent-up frustration because she did me in. I was ready to fight this bitch for real. I reached in my purse and counted out five one-hundred-dollar bills and handed them to Kesha

"Thanks, bitch," I said.

"No problem, shit anytime you need me to beat that ass again you know where you can find me," she said.

"Girl chill because if we were really fighting, you would be picking your teeth up off the damn floor, "I said.

I grabbed my purse, threw a pair of shades over my face, and walked the fuck up out of her pissy ass project. I drove back to Sin's and called the police.

Kyra

I was being discharged from the hospital. Instead of calling Denise or Dinero, I called my mom asking her to pick me up.

“Thanks for coming to get me, ma,” I said, turning my head looking out the window.

“Girl, it’s nothing. Why didn't you call Dinero? You two fighting again?” she asked. I let out a huge sigh.

“Ma, Dinero cheated on me with some chick he used to date,” I said. My mom looked over at me.

“Oh my,” she said.

“Yep, the whole time I was laying on that ground and Denise was trying to call him, he was sexing some chick,” I said. “And to top it off he came to the hospital with evidence all on his clothes, plus somebody sent a video to my phone,” I said, trying to hold back tears.

“Not that I’m taking up for Dinero because what he did was wrong, but think about it, Kyra. You said somebody sent a video to your phone, which means somebody set him up. Who would record something like that and send to you if they weren’t trying to start something? One thing you got to learn honey is misery loves company. If they can’t be happy, they don’t want nobody else to be. You gone do what you want to, but just think about it before you make a hasty decision. I remember when your father cheated on me,” ma said. I looked at her because I had always known for my mother and father to be the perfect happy couple.

"Daddy cheated on you?" I asked. My mom nodded her head

"Yep, sure did with this girl name Monica Jenkins. I had just found out I was pregnant with you, and I went to his house to tell him the news. When I got there, he acted like he ain't want to let me in so I knew then it was some shit in the game. I pulled my .22 out and ran up in his house. I caught the little bitch putting her clothes on," ma said.

I was cracking up because I had never heard this and my mother was this holy roly woman so to hear her talk like this about her, and my daddy was hilarious.

"I shot your daddy in his leg, that's where that limp came from so that lie about him getting hurt on his job isn't true. I didn't shoot Monica, but I did whoop her ass real good. I stopped talking to your daddy for some months, but he never gave up. He swore he would never cheat on me again for as long as he lived. I'm still holding him to that," ma said. I laughed and shook my head.

"Am I taking you home, or are you coming to the house with me?" ma asked.

"You can take me home," I said.

Pulling into the yard, I knew Dinero was home because his cars where in the yard, and my car was there also. Mama came around and helped me get out the car. I could walk fine; my leg was just bandaged up from the bullet graze. We walked up the stairs to the door, and I used my key to open the door. Dinero came walking out of the kitchen carrying a sandwich.

"Hey ma," he said as if I wasn't standing there.

"Hey Dinero," my mother said and turned to me as Dinero walked off to his office.

"Damn, did I cheat or him? He's walking around like I did something to him," I said to my mom.

"Kyra, y'all need to have a sit down maybe he just trying to give you your space. I don't know, but I'm gone get out y'all hair. Call me if you need anything," ma said, kissing me on my cheek. She turned around heading back out the door, and I locked the door behind her.

I walked towards Dinero office and didn't bother knocking. I just walked right on in. "You ever heard of knocking? That's the polite thing to do." Dinero looked up gazing at me. Not breaking our stare

"When have I ever knocked on that door? You tripping, where is Dinelle?" I asked.

"I just laid her down for a nap," Dinero said. He continued to look at me like he had something he wanted to say

"You got something on your chest that you need to get off? What's with the attitude? I'm the one should be walking around here with an attitude. Your little video looked real nice by the way. I see you have a future in the porn industry," I said. I saw Dinero jaw twitch. I knew he was getting pissed.

"Were you ever gone tell me you told Nitro about the baby?" he asked, throwing me off. I shook my head Denise snitching ass.

"No, I wasn't. For one the nigga ran up on me at a place that I thought I was safe at. Somebody at Trev's told that nigga that I be there often and whoever it was knew that I was carrying his child. The only person knew that was Trev, Bianca and us. Nothing fucking happened between me and my ex though. I told him I was carrying his child, but I was with you and that y'all had too much shit going on. Now he came up to the hospital to check on me, and I'm sure Denise the one told you all this shit. So, you can sit here and be mad all you want. I honestly don't care. You, on the other hand, got a lot of making up to do because I came in here trying to forgive you for this bullshit that you did. You could've turned away from Ivy, but you didn't," I said. Dinero stood up from his desk and walked around to me.

"I told you I was sorry for that, but you can't be out here playing both sides. You either riding with me or you can go attempt to raise your kid with Nitro, even though that won't last long once I get a hold of him," Dinero said. I leaned my head back shocked at the shit he just said.

"Really Dinero, playing both sides, but where the fuck am I? I'm standing right here with you. I told Dinero I was with you and things wasn't changing. But, I now see how it is," I said, turning to walk away.

The doorbell rang, and I headed to the door. “Who is it?” I yelled.

“Police.” I unlocked the door and opened it.

“How can I help you?” I asked the officers.

“We're looking for a Dinero Jackson, does he by any chance live here?” the officers asked. I heard Dinero coming from behind me.

“What seems to be the problem officer?” Dinero asked.

“Are you Dinero Jackson?” the officer asked.

“Yes,” Dinero said.

“Sir, you are under arrest for the assault and battery of a Tori Santiago,” the other office said while placing cuffs on Dinero.

“What the fuck, I ain’t even seen that girl. She just shot my girl yesterday!” Dinero yelled.

“Perfect reason for you to seek revenge, huh?” the white officer said. I looked at Dinero and mouthed, “What did you do?” he shook his head.

“I swear I ain’t seen that girl in forever. Call Anderson and tell him,” Dinero said before being placed in the back of the police car.

I stood in the doorway and watched as they took my man off to jail. I closed the door and headed to Dinero’s office and found Anderson’s number. Anderson was Dinero’s lawyer. This bitch Tori was becoming a damn problem. I picked up the phone and dialed Anderson's cell number.

"Anderson," he said.

"Hello Anderson, this is Kyra Mitchell. I'm calling on behalf of Dinero Jackson." I said.

"Oh yes, I hope he hasn't gotten himself in any trouble," Anderson said.

"Well see he was just picked up from the house on an assault and battery charge from his ex-girlfriend Tori Santiago. The thing is I was shot yesterday by this same person, and I know for a fact that whatever she's saying he did is a lie," I said.

"Ok, I see. I'm gone head on down to the station and check out all the details, and I will call you," Anderson said.

"Ok, thank you," I said, ending the call. I placed the phone on the desk and headed to Dinelle's room to check on her.

Chapter 14

Nitro

“So, this where that nigga stays at?” I turned and asked Turk. Turk nodded his head

“Yep, and she stay here with him,” he said. I shook my head. “I can’t believe this whole time that this nigga was Tori brother. I swear I wish I had of never fucked with that low life having ass bitch. She gone wish she hadn’t of fucked with Nitro,” I said.

We sat in the car watching the apartment and the traffic of people outside. I screwed the silencer on and tucked it in my waistband. Turk’s phone started ringing

“Yeah,” he answered.

“Aite, cool. Bet,” he said and hung up the phone.

“The drop is going down tomorrow; that was Lanez,” Turk said.

“That’s what’s up, good looking out on that for me,” I said. “Aite, let’s ride,” I said, hopping out of the car.

I made my way across the parking lot. I spotted the black BMW I was told Tori had, so I knew she was in here. Turk and I skipped up the stairs headed towards Sin’s apartment. I stood on one side of the door while Turk knocked on the door.

“Who is it?” I heard Tori yell.

“Turk,” Turk said. Tori opened the door.

“Ugh boy, what you want?” Tori asked.

“I know you want me. I don’t know why you be playing. Where’s Sin at?” Turk asked.

“He ran to the store to get some cigars, you can come in and wait,” Tori said turning around while Turk followed her in the house. I came in right behind Turk. I closed the door and locked it.

“Tori, Tori,” I said. “Girl you can’t just be letting folks in the house like that,” I said. Tori turned around and locked eyes with me

“What the fuck you want?” she asked. I shook my head.

“You just out here fucking shit up not thinking about the consequences. But you stepped on my toes when you tried to harm my seed,” Nitro said. Tori rolled her eyes.

“Nobody cares about Kyra. You and Dinero both out here looking like damn fools for what? That bitch can’t see me on her worse day. You think I care anything about the next bitch baby when you damn near beat my baby out of me. So, fuck you, Kyra, and that bastard ass baby. Fuck all y’all.”

PEW! PEW!

I let off two shots to her head and watched Tori fall to the floor. I placed the gun back in my waist and walked out of the apartment with Turk right behind me.

Kyra

I was half done packing up Dinelle and my things. Last night after the few words Dinero and me had, I had come to the conclusion that it was best for me to go. I wanted to stay and work things out with him, but him saying I was playing both sides were basically saying he didn't trust me as long as I was carrying the next man's baby. Dinelle was sitting in the living room playing with her dolls. I really hated to take my baby out the home with her father. I always wanted my kids to grow up with both parents in the home. I stared at my daughter. She looked just like her father. She had his chocolate skin and thick full lips. His round eyes and my curly hair. I smiled. The doorbell rang. I placed the shirt I had in my hand in the box and walked to the door.

Opening the door there stood Denise. I sighed. "Well hi to you too, bitch," Denise said, walking in the house.

"Denise, what do you want?" I asked not excited to see her at all. She walked over to Dinelle and picked her up.

"Look, I know I said some fucked up shit yesterday, but it needed to be said. Y'all moving? Denise asked looking around at some of the things I had packed. I crossed my arms.

"Dinelle and I are leaving. Thanks to what you told Dinero yesterday, he thinks I'm playing both sides. Even though I know he said pick, he shouldn't even have let that come out of his mouth because I was here. I came back to my home that we shared. Willing to work things out after his little sexcapade, and he stills say some shit like that me. I need some space. I'm so over everything and all this fucking drama that I got to deal with just because I want to be with the man I love. I swear this shit is draining me." I sat on the couch and placed my head in my hands and cried. Denise placed Dinelle back on the floor and came over to console me.

"I'm so sorry Kyra, I really am. I want nothing more for you and my brother to finally be together. Just seeing Nitro rubbed me the wrong way. I know you would never hurt my brother, but if you leave now who's to say what may happen with y'all," Denise said. I lifted my head.

"I would never leave him while he is going through this shit, I'm still gone be here for him, but I just need some time. This baby is complicating things. I wish I had of never gotten pregnant," I admitted.

"Don't say that, Kyra. God has his way of showing us things. I don't know exactly what he's trying to show y'all yet, but things happen for a reason. Regardless of who the daddy is, that child is still a part of you, Kyra," Denise said.

My phone beeped, and I looked down, and it was Anderson.

"Hello," I answered quickly.

"Baby, it's me Dinero," Dinero's voice boomed through the phone

"Are you out?" I asked.

“Nah, shit is looking fucked up. I’m innocent though. I ain’t never put my hands on Tori, let alone seen her ass. They showed me the pics of what she claimed I did. This bitch had to hire somebody to do that to her. Another thing, the police went to her house for more questioning and found her dead, Kyra,” Dinero said. I smiled.

“Damn that’s messed up,” I said.

“Yeah it is, seeing that they’re trying to say I had something to do with that too,” Dinero said.

“WHAT THE FUCK??” I yelled.

“Baby calm down, one thing I know is the truth and Anderson is working hard on this. Trust me when I say I will be home soon. But check this out, I need a huge favor. Call David; he’s got some directions for you. I never asked you for anything, but I need you to handle this for me.” Next time I call, it most likely will be from the jail phone. I love you, Ky,” Dinero said.

“I love you too,” I said and ended the call.

“What?” Denise asked.

“Tori was found dead, and now they’re thinking your brother had something to do with it,” I told Denise.

“Yeah fucking right,” Denise said.

“I wish I was playing. He said don’t worry about it though because he had nothing to do with none of this shit,” I said. I looked at my phone and dialed David.

"David, what's up?" I said.

"Come thru; I'm gone text you the address," he said.

"Ok," I said, ending the call.

"I got to take care of something for your brother. Can you watch Dinelle for me please?" I asked.

"Sure. Come here TT baby." Denise said, picking up Dinelle again.

I ran upstairs and hopped in the shower. I lathered up my body with Bath and Body Works Twilight Woods shower gel. I closed my eyes and thought about everything. Now I knew I couldn't leave Dinero, not like this. Will we be ok when he comes home? I rinsed the soap off my body and grabbed a towel to dry off walking out of the shower. Drying off, I then applied some coconut oil to my stomach and body. I got dressed and waited for David to text me the address. When the address came through, I headed downstairs to my safe and removed my gun. I then walked into the living room and kissed Dinelle before heading out the door.

The address was taking me to The Gulch. It took me about fifteen minutes to get there from our home. I pulled up to the building. I saw David car, so I hopped out and headed to the door. When I got to the door, David was walking towards me, and he unlocked the door.

"Hey, David. What is all this?" I asked, looking around at all the designer fashion in men and women's.

"This here is your shop," he said. I whipped my head and lifted my brow.

"My shop? What are you talking about?" I asked him. He laughed.

"Did you even bother reading the sign when you pulled up?" he asked. He handed me what looked like a flyer that said *Kyra's High Fashion.*

"This is all Dinero's doing. This is your shop to do whatever you want with it. It's all yours," David said.

I wanted to cry because this was the sweetest thing someone had ever done for me. I had something of my own, no longer having to work for somebody else.

"Now that that's out the way we need to discuss why Dinero really wanted you to come down here," David said.

David walked off heading to the back, and I followed him. We entered an office, and I was greeted by two guys, one I knew was Denise's boyfriend the other I wasn't familiar with.

"This is Turk, and of course you know Lanez. Tonight, we're setting up a lick with your boy Nitro. Turk and Lanez are going to go meet up with him and hit one of our traps. The trap he hits has fake kilos and counterfeit bills," David said. I still had no clue as to why I was called down here.

"So, where do I come in at in all of this?" I asked.

“Sniper skills boo, you can finally put all that training to work,” David said.

I stood there taking in all he had just said. Dinero really wanted me to kill Nitro. I guess this was him using me to prove who I wanted to be with. I didn’t want to kill Nitro, but I didn’t want to be with him either. I sighed.

“What do I have to do?” I asked. David smiled.

“There’s an abandon apartment located across the street. It’s the perfect sniper position; I found it myself,” David said.

“Cool, I’m ready,” I said.

Chapter 15

Nitro

This is what I had been waiting for another big ass lick. I looked out the window thinking how when I get this shit, a nigga would be set, and I'm relocating to Atlanta. Of course, after Kyra has the baby. I didn't want to miss that for that world.

"You know how many niggas he gone have here?" I asked Turk.

"My homie said only one. After them losses he took at the other traps, he didn't want a lot of people in one house," Turk said. Nitro was thinking how this shit sounded too good to be true. All this shit at one spot.

"Why this nigga got this much shit at one spot tho?" I asked Turk.

"Because everyone knows he stash a certain amount at each spot, so he had to switch that shit up," Turk said. I nodded my head. I guess he had a point.

We parked a couple of house down from the spot.

"Aite, let's go," I said, stepping out the car.

I looked at the house. This was a different crib and a nice neighborhood. Yeah, he switched it up big time. I walked around back to the kitchen door and peeked in the house. I saw a nigga walking around with his phone up to his ear. I heard the doorbell ring, and I knew that was Turk and Lanez making the distraction. Once I saw them enter the house, I picked the lock on the back door and let myself in with ease.

"That was too damn easy," I said. I made my way from the kitchen to the living room where Turk had dude tied up.

"Just tell me where the stash at, and I'm out your hair," I said.

"Man, that shit in the bathroom behind the toilet in the wall," he said quickly as fuck. I shook my head.

"Dinero needs to get some more killas to guard his possessions." I chuckled and walked off heading towards the bathroom.

I walked into the bathroom and looked behind the toilet at the wall trying to see if I could tell which part had been messed with. I use the butt of my gun to knock on pieces until a piece popped out and I removed it. My eyes lit up at the shit I was looking at in the wall—bricks, and cash. I grabbed all that shit.

Kyra

I stood across the street in the window. I had watch Turk, Nitro, and Lanez get out the Crown Vic. Nitro took off around back while Turk and Lanez went through the front door. My nerves were getting the best of me because I was about to kill Nitro. I looked at my phone, and it was a text from Turk.

We about to come out.

I laid the phone on the floor next to my bag and continued to look out the window with my sniper rifle ready.

"Come on, come on," I said to nobody in particular.

I saw the door open to the house and all of sudden I felt a hand cover my mouth and grab me forcefully away from the window. I was kicking but couldn't scream out. I felt myself losing strength, and I was dragged out the apartment building.

Turk

Opening the front door and making my way outside with Nitro and Lanez following behind me. I knew in a matter of minutes that Nitro ass would be laid out in cold blood. I looked over at the apartment that I knew Kyra was looking out of the window and nodded my head. I looked at Nitro making his way over to the car but still no shot.

"Aye, put that in the trunk!" I yelled at Nitro trying to buy some more time.

I watched as he made his way to the back and still nothing. I looked at Lanez, and he shrugged like he ain't know what the hell was going on either. Why the fuck this nigga ain't been shot yet. We hopped in the car and sped back to Nitro's place. Dammit Kyra, now shit was really fucked up. She had plenty times to shoot that nigga why the fuck she didn't. I couldn't call David until Nitro was out the car. I pulled at Nitro's and popped the trunk. "I'll be by later to pick up my cut, I got to go check on my girl," I said.

"Aite, hit my line nigga," Nitro said, stepping out the car. I watched as he removed the bag from the trunk and walked in the house.

"Man, what the fuck just happened?" Lanez asking, hopping in the front seat.

"Nigga, I don't even know. Let me call David," I said.

I grabbed my phone and dialed David. I was sitting at the light, and this nigga wasn't answering. My line beeped.

"Yeah," I answered.

"Man, where you at I need somebody to come and scoop me. 'I'm out," Dinero said.

"I'm on my way," I said, ending the call. I busted a U-turn and headed to the jail to pick up Dinero.

"That nigga David ain't answering but that was Dinero, he's out," I said. I decided to call Kyra's phone. "Bruh, why the fuck ain't nobody answering they damn phone.

I pulled up at the jail and Dinero was waiting outside. Dinero hopped in.

"Preciate it man, what's good. How did everything go down?" Dinero asked. I sighed not wanting to tell Dinero the news.

"Kyra never fired the shot. I don't know what happened. We came out the house and set the shot up when I didn't see that nigga hit the ground I tried to get her another clear shot by telling him to put the shit in the trunk. He did that but still no shot I called David's phone and Kyra's, but nobody is fucking answering," Turk said.

Dinero

What the fuck man? I set up a simple and smooth take out of this nigga, and the job still doesn't get done. I had tried calling David and Kyra but still no answer. "Go back to the apartment!" I yelled. I was beyond pissed, but now I was getting worried. I called my sister.

"Hello," she answered.

"Hey, you ain't talked to Kyra, have you?" I asked.

"Nah, she's been gone for a minute. I'm still here watching Dinelle," Denise said.

"Is everything ok?" she asked.

"Yeah, if she calls tell her I'm home," I said, disconnecting the call.

We pulled up at the spot and hopped out the car. "Do you know which apartment it was?" I asked Turk.

"I just know that nigga said the third-floor window," Turk said.

I turned and headed inside the apartment building, a lot of the apartments in this building was vacant. It looks to be an abandoned building. I walked up to the third floor.

It's got to be one of these two apartments; it's the only two with windows on this floor.

I turned the knob to the first door, Turk and Lanez had their guns drawn ready to drop anything in sight. When I opened the door, I saw a bag and gun left on the floor. I ran over to the window where Kyra had been standing. I bent down and picked up her phone that was laying on the bag.

"Fuck man!" I yelled. "This shit's not looking right and somebody better start fucking talking!" I yelled, looking at Turk and Lanez.

"Nigga, we're just as lost as you. The only other person that knew she was here was David's ass, and he not answering his phone," Lanez said.

"And Nitro was with y'all the whole time?" I asked.

"Yeah and I dropped that nigga off," Turk said. I didn't want to think negative because David was my nigga. I just refuse to believe he had anything to do with Kyra's disappearance.

Nitro

A nigga was laid out on the bed feeling good. I had just counted all the money, and I had a good half a mill sitting in there of cash and bricks. My phone rang and I answered.

"Yeah, what up Sin?" I asked.

"I got somebody that wants to talk to you," he said.

"Nitro, please help me!" I heard the fear in Kyra's voice.

"Sin, nigga, you done lost your motherfucking mind?" I asked.

"I haven't lost shit yet, I'm gone do away with this bitch if you're not here in thirty minutes with everything you got from that little lick you hit. 2764 Brooks Avenue, thirty minutes," he said and ended the call.

"Shit!" I yelled, throwing the phone on the bed.

I threw my clothes back on and headed to the living room to bag all the shit up. I wasn't stuttin' Kyra; I didn't want shit to happen to her while she was carrying my baby.

I ran to my car and put the address in my GPS and hit go. I was swerving in and out of traffic. I hated Nashville here it was ten o'clock at night, and it's fucking traffic. I tapped my hand on the steering wheel because my nerves were getting the best of me now. I took my exit and followed the directions the rest of the way. I arrived at the destination and grabbed the bag and exited the car. I ran up the steps and started banging on the door. Sin opened the door. I should've shot his ass right there, but I needed to get Kyra first.

"I knew you wouldn't disappoint me," Sin said, letting me in.

"Where's Kyra?" I asked not seeing her anywhere.

"Kyra is fine; I'll bring her out in a minute.

"Nigga, if you want what's in this bag, you better bring her ass in here so that I can see her. I'm not about to play these games with you," I said.

"First off nigga, you not calling the shots," Sin said.

I unzipped the bag showing him I had what he wanted. Then I zipped it back up. Sin turned around and walked off to another room. I smiled. I stood there checking out the place and my surroundings. Sin came back in the room pushing Kyra. Her mouth was tied up, and she had been crying. I hated seeing her like that. I grew hot.

"Hand me the bag, and you can have this cry baby here, she's been working my nerves anyway," Sin said.

"Same time," I said. I dropped the bag and slid it across the floor.

Sin pushed Kyra towards me, and I reached my hand out for Kyra, and she ran and grabbed it. I pushed her behind me. Sin picked up the bag and looked at it eyeballing the money and the keys. He removed the money from the bag going through each stack. Satisfied with what was in the bag he looked up.

"I guess now I can head back to New York and bury my sister. I know you killed her. Yeah, she was a bitch but all she ever wanted for some damn reason was to be loved. The one thing she was going to love you took from her. Oh, and Kyra you need to tell Dinero if you ever see him again that his nigga David is as big of a snake as this nigga here. How you think I knew where you were," Sin said.

POP!

"Niggas talk too much," David said. Sin hit the floor.

"I gave this nigga one job. Niggas like to get greedy I don't know where he was going with all that fake shit," David said. I looked at David like he was crazy.

"Nigga, you were set up. All that shit was fake— the money and the coke," David said. Kyra was about to kill your ass, but I stopped that." David said.

I turned to look at Kyra removing the tie from her mouth. "You were gone kill me?" I asked.

Her answer spoke volumes when she didn't speak. I turned back around to face David. He had his gun pointed at me.

"Now I'm just gone kill both of y'all," he said.

POP! POP!

David hit the floor. I turned around and looked at Kyra with the smoking gun in her still tied hands. I grabbed the gun out of her hand. "So, you knew that your nigga was setting me up?" I asked her.

"I didn't know shit until I was asked to take you out," Kyra said.

I walked over to the bags and looked at the shit, this shit looked real as hell. It was no way this shit could be fake. "It's fake, Nitro," Kyra said.

I stood up and walked over to her hitting her in the face with the butt of the gun. "Bitch, I ought to kill your ass just because. You really love that nigga, don't you?" I asked. Kyra spit blood out of her mouth in my face.

"You damn right I love him, always have and always will. You don't know how to love anybody, Nitro. You use people only for your needs. From the time, I met your ass you knew you was coming in to fuck up my life. I hate you; I wish I never met you. I swear if I make it out of this alive, my son will never grow up to be anything like your twisted crazy ass!" Kyra yelled.

"Fuck you. I'm gone make sure you never see Dinero ass again!" I yelled, dragging Kyra to the car.

Chapter 16

Dinero

Four months later

"Dinero, wake up!" I heard my sister yelling my name. I rolled over.

"What?" I groaned.

"You need to get the hell up and get your life. I already took Dinelle to daycare for you, but something's got to give, bruh," Denise said.

I picked the pillow up and placed it over my head trying to tune out everything she was saying. Denise grabbed the pillow.

"Get the fuck up Dinero!" she yelled, smacking me with the pillow.

"Aite damn, chill out," I said, swinging my feet around and sitting on the edge of the bed.

I scratched my beard; that shit felt rough. I knew it was rough. I couldn't tell you the last time I went to the barbershop. A nigga's been fucked up these last four months without Kyra. It's like she vanished off the face of the earth. I felt she ran off to be with Nitro when a nigga came back home. That night she went missing she had packed up a lot of her Dinelle's things. Denise told me about the talk they had, so I knew deep down she was riding for a nigga. I had done everything I could to look for Kyra. I knew she was with Nitro because

David and Sin were both found dead with the dummy bag that I had set up for Nitro. Turk said he knew for a fact that Nitro took the bag, so this nigga's around here somewhere with my woman. I found myself most nights going back to the abandoned apartment where she last was at. I would just sit there in silence. I can't believe I let David talk me into letting Kyra take Nitro out.

I walked in the bathroom and hopped in the shower. I stood in the shower and just let the water run over me. Placing my hands on the wall in front of me I prayed for the first time in a long time.

God, I don't ask for much, but I feel like a part of me has died without my other half. I need her. I can't be who I need to be without her. I need my rib. I'm sorry for everything I ever took her through. Just give me my girl back and let her be ok. Amen.

I finished washing up and hopped out the shower. I wrapped the towel around my waist and walked into the closet. I looked at Kyra's side. I couldn't bring myself to touch anything of hers. She was coming back, so I left everything like she had it. I unpacked all her shit and hung it back up. I turned to my side and grabbed a Tru Religion jogger set and shirt to put on. Once I got dressed, I headed downstairs Denise and Lanez where in the kitchen having breakfast. I rolled my eyes.

"Can't y'all do that shit at your crib?" I asked. Denise smacked her mouth. I knew she was about to say something smart.

"I will go back to my crib when you get your shit together," Denise said. "You have a child to care for, and she can't be round here wondering what the hell wrong with her daddy," Denise said.

I texted my barber asking him could I come through today to get a cut. After stuffing my face with the breakfast that Denise had cooked, I left the house. I hit the interstate heading back to town. I had the radio on XM radio vibing to the sounds that came through the speakers. I damn near lost my mind when Kyra and I song came on Faith Evan's "Soon As I Get Home".

That song alone brought out so many damn emotions, but I also took it as sign from God. Every time Kyra left, for whatever reason this song came on. When she went to camp our middle school year, she sang this song to me. She came back. The day before she got locked up this song came on the radio; she came back. When she got out, and she got drunk as hell and was singing this song at her party, she knew all along that she was coming back to me and we would make up lost time. Hearing this song now, I knew my girl was coming back. I wiped the tear that fell down my cheek. I swear if it took my own life. Nitro was gone have to die.

Kyra

Sitting in the bed watching reruns of *Love & Hip Hop*, I grew irritated because it wasn't shit on TV. I had watched enough TV for the past four months that I could act out every show and win a fucking Grammy. I have no clue where I'm at. Nitro kept me locked away in this damn room. I knew my time was coming to an end. He always would say as soon you have that baby I'm gone kill your ass. He kept me fed. Whoever the chef was could cook because whatever I had a taste for I tell Nitro, and he sends it to my room. I looked down at my round belly. I knew I was coming close to my due date. I ran my hand over my stomach. I heard keys on the other side of the door, so I knew somebody was coming in. In walked Nurse Gabby.

"Hello, mamacita," Gabby spoke. She was an older Mexican lady. She was a nurse that Nitro kept on call for me.

"Hey, Gabby," I said.

Every time she came in the room, I would try to pick her by asking her questions, but she would never budge. Gabby walked over to the bed where I was sitting, and she had a look of concern on her face.

"I was told to you give you this shot, it will do no harm to your baby," she said, shaking her head. I smacked her hand.

"Wait a damn minute. What is that?" I asked.

"It's Oxytocin; it will jumpstart your labor," she said.

"Ms. Gabby, don't do this. Look, how much is he paying you? If you can help me, I can triple that. All you have to do is get me a phone in here and at least tell me where we at," I pleaded.

"I'll see what I can do, but I must hurry and give—" Gabby was cut off mid-sentence.

"What the hell is taking you so long, Gabby? I asked you to do one thing and leave this room," Nitro said.

"I asked her what the hell she was giving me," I said. I was so over Nitro, and he didn't scare me at all. I turned to look at Gabby with pleading eyes while she gave me the shot of Oxytocin. She tapped my hand when she was finished and left the room.

Nitro came and sat down on the bed beside me rubbing his hands across my stomach. "I'll see you soon, son."

Instantly my child kicked. He had gotten accustomed to hearing Nitro's voice. Nitro would come and talk to the baby every day. It was crazy to see a softer side of him when it came to his child, but then he goes right back to his maniac ways when dealing with me. I hated for Nitro to touch me period. I would just lay there and let him have his way with me. I had gotten numb to the fact of the things he did to me over time. I dozed off trying to dream at least some happy thoughts.

"Kyra," I heard my name being whispered. I opened my eyes, and I saw Ms. Gabby standing there.

"I slid a phone under your pillow. That's all I could do. My number is in the phone so when and if you get out of here. I will be expecting my money," she said.

I smiled, but at the same, I thought this little wench was all about money. "Thank you," I said.

"Ouch!" I said, grabbing my stomach.

"Oh, mamacita, I think the time has come. The contractions will be more and more frequent. I'm gone to hook you up to this monitor to keep watch on your contractions and the baby," Ms. Gabby said. I nodded my head. "Every time you get a contraction I want you to relax and try to breathe through it, ok?" she said.

"Yeah, ok," I said.

* * *

It had been about three hours, and the contractions were getting worse by the minute.

"Ms. Gabby, I can't take this shit. Can you please give me something for pain?" I yelled. Nitro walked in the room clutching his cigar.

"Is she ready to push yet?" he asked. Ms. Gabby looked at Nitro.

"Boy, when the time comes for her to push, I will let you know. Hopefully, this baby won't have to be cut out," Gabby said.

"You better pray this baby doesn't have to get cut out because he is coming out today regardless. I don't care if I have to bury you right along with her ass," Nitro said before turning to walk back out the room. "I fucking hate you!" I yelled loud enough so he could hear every word.

"I hate you too!" I heard him yell.

The pain was excruciating. I laid my head back on the pillow while Ms. Gabby dabbed my face with a wet cloth.

"You should be able to push in a few minutes," Gabby said.

"The phone; I've got to make a call before Nitro comes back in here," I said. Ms. Gabby slid me the phone, and I dialed Dinero's number. I instantly started crying when I heard Dinero's voice.

"Ky, is that you?" I heard him asked.

"Yes, I don't have much time, but Nitro has got me locked up somewhere. I have no clue where I'm at, and I've been in this damn room for four months. I'm about to have this baby. He's going to kill me when I have him. I won't hang the phone up, but I'm gone hide it. Please try and track this call," I whispered all in one breathe.

"Ok baby, I got you. I'm on it," Dinero said. I gave the phone back to Ms. Gabby, and she slid it back under the pillow.

Dinero

I had just left the barbershop when I got a call from a number I didn't know. I never answered numbers I didn't know, but something told me to answer. And I'm glad I did. Hearing Kyra's voice lit a fire in me that had died. I was on fixed time, and I had to find her as soon as possible. I grabbed my other phone and put in a call to my homie Dexter. He was a computer geek and could break into anything.

"Aye, yo, Dex, I need a phone traced for a location. It's life or death situation," I said. "Ok, buddy I gotcha give me the number," Dex said.

"555-552-3456," I said, calling the number off.

"She said she was leaving the phone on." I said.

"Ok, that's great. Let me run some things here," Dex said. I heard him typing away on his computer. I was tired of waiting, so as soon as I got an address, I was heading to get my woman.

"Ok, looks like I got something here. It's showing a tower in Bowling Green, Kentucky. If you give me about five minutes I can get an actual address and send it to your phone," Dex said.

"Ok, Preciate that. I got you when I get back," I said. I disconnected the call and called Turk.

"What up, bro?" Turk yelled. It was loud as hell in the background.

"Nigga, I need you to go with me and get Kyra," I said.

"Oh word, do I need to bring artillery?" he asked.

"Hell yeah," I said. "Cool, I'm at the crib," Turk said. I headed straight to Turk's. I was going to get my woman.

Chapter 17

Kyra

"Give me one more push, Ms. Kyra!" Ms. Gabby yelled at me.

I was growing weak. I barely had the strength to get this baby out of me. Nitro stood off to the side watching everything take place. I lifted my head and grunted down giving one last push before I heard the cries of my son.

"It's a boy," I heard Ms. Gabby say.

She wrapped the baby up in a blanket and laid him on my chest. I looked at my son and instantly wanted to smile at what I was seeing, but the fear in what Nitro would do to my child is what scared me the most. I was looking at a spitting image of Dinelle and Dinero. I must have been off on my conception because this baby was Dinero's. Nitro walked over to the bed. I tighten my grip on my son.

"Ms. Kyra, you're losing a lot of blood," she said worried she looked at the machine that I was hooked up to and checked my blood pressure.

"Her blood pressure is dropping, and she's losing way too much blood, she needs to get to a hospital ASAP before she goes into shock!" Ms. Gabby was yelling at Nitro.

Nitro grabbed my baby out of my arms, and I couldn't even put up a fight because I was getting weak.

"You ready to go with daddy?" I heard him ask my son. "Let's go, she can die for all I care," Nitro said, turning around to make his exit out the door. Ms. Gabby made her way to my side of the bed and grabbed the phone that was under my pillow. She hung up the phone and dialed 911. She squeezed my hand and left out the room.

"It's not his baby!" I said. I thought I had yelled, but no one could hear me. I could hear the operator on the phone. "Help, he took my baby and, and…" was all I could get out before I blacked out.

Nitro

I held my son in my arms and looked at his tiny body. Placing him carefully in the car seat, I buckled him in. "Ma, let's go the plane is waiting!" I yelled.

Ms. Gabby walked into the room wearing a smug look on her face. "I can't believe you are doing this to that girl. I didn't raise you like this, Nathanial." Gabby said.

"You're right you didn't raise me at all," I said.

Gabby was my Mexican mother; she had me and gave me to my father. My dad was as black as they come. I resented my mother sometimes for her not being there like she should, but her family wasn't cool with the fact that she was pregnant by a black man. I picked up the car seat and looked back at my mother. "Let's go ma, I'm not gone tell you again," I said. she shook her head and followed me to the plane.

Boarding the private jet, I placed my son in the seat next to me. I watched as my mom boarded the plane. She took the seat across from me. “What are you going to name him?” she asked.

“He will be a Jr.,” I said.

“Have you even thought this out. How are you gone get away with this if she survives? That woman is not gone let you get away with this. That is her child and one thing I know about a mother and her cubs, she does whatever she has to do to protect them,” Gabby said.

I just looked at her and didn’t respond. I was heading to Atlanta to start a life with my son, and I wasn’t trying to hear shit my mother said.

Dínero

I pulled up at the address that Dex gave me, and I saw police cars. Turk and I left the guns in the car and ran up to the house.

“Sir, you can’t go in there,” one of the officers told me. “The girl that was here, please tell is me she ok?” I asked.

“How do you know the woman?” the officer asked.

“She’s my girlfriend. Her ex kidnaped her, and she called me today saying that he was gone kill her after she had the baby,” I said. The officer looked at me like I was crazy

“So, you are telling me she was kidnapped but just now calling you to tell you where she was at?” he asked. I was getting pissed and felt myself about to go off on this officer.

“Excuse me; I’m Detective Tully, I’m working this case. Sorry for that,” he said, pointing at the officer.

“Is Kyra ok?” I asked.

“She looks to be fine. They got her stabilize before taking her to the hospital. We had to get her there right away. If someone hadn’t called when they did, she probably would’ve died. Do you have any idea who would do this to her? Because from the looks of inside it was a makeshift birthing room. There are signs that a birth indeed took place, but no signs of a baby.” The officer was telling me so much stuff that my head was spinning.

“We were going to put an amber alert on the child, but there’s no vehicle plus she was too out of it to give a description of the baby,” the detective told me.

“I appreciate it. Can I get the address to the hospital?” I asked.

“Sure, follow me,” Detective Tully said. I followed him to his squad car and retrieved the address.

After getting the hospital address from the detective, I was on my way to my girl.

“Man, this nigga is sick as fuck. How can you leave somebody like that and then take a baby? I can’t wait to see that nigga.” Turk said.

“Nigga, who you telling,” I said.

After about fifteen minutes, we arrived at Tri-Star Greenview Regional Hospital. I parked the car and ran into the hospital with Turk on my heels. I saw two nurses sitting in the emergency area, so I went to them.

“Yeah, I’m looking for a Kyra Mitchell she was brought in here after delivering a baby that’s missing.” The nurse nodded her head

“Yes, I remember her. Follow me,” the nurse said. I followed the nurse to Kyra’s room. The nurse turned to me

“This story is so heartbreaking, but she is very strong, she wasn’t supposed to survive this. Thank God she called the police. The main concern now is monitoring her blood pressure. I know she is ready to go home so she can find her baby, but make sure you keep her calm,” the nurse said.

“Thank you, ma’am,” I said.

I opened the door to Kyra’s room, and she was there looking peaceful as ever. I slowly stepped over to her not wanting to wake her. I wanted to take this moment in. Not seeing her all those months, a nigga thought I lost her for good. I used my hand to brush her hair out her face. She stirred and slowly opened her eyes.

“Am I dreaming?” she asked. I picked up her hand and kissed it.

“No baby, it’s real. I’m here and not going nowhere,” I said. Tears started rolling down her face.

“Kyra, look, baby, you got to remain calm so that your blood pressure doesn’t go back up,” I told her, trying to make sure she understood what I was saying. She nodded her head.

“The baby isn’t Nitro’s,” she whispered.

“What?” I asked to make sure I heard her right.

“The baby, he is your baby. He looks just like you and Dinelle,” she said. I closed my eyes and ran my hands over my face. This shit was most definitely about to get ugly now. I looked back at Kyra.

“How did you get a phone?” I asked. He had a nurse that stayed there with us. Her name’s Gabby; she helped me,” she said.

“You never heard him talking about where he might go?” I asked her.

“No, he kept me in that room locked up. Hell, I couldn’t even see if it was night or day outside. It felt like prison all over again,” she said.

“We gone find our son, I promise you that,” I told her reassuring her.

Kyra

Two days of being cooped up in the hospital was enough for me. We were finally heading back to Nashville. I couldn't wait to see my daughter. I prayed that soon I would get to bring my son home also. Turk was in the backseat stretched out snoring his ass off. I looked over at Dinero. I could tell he had a million things on his mind.

"I never got to tell you thank you for my shop," I said.

"It's nothing baby. It's all yours," he said. "Not that it matters because I killed him, but David was the one behind me being kidnapped," I told Dinero. This was my first time speaking about it since it happened. Dinero looked at me.

"You killed David?" he asked me.

"Yeah, he was about to shoot Nitro. I have no clue why I saved him, but if I hadn't both of us would've died," I said.

"Well, a nigga will never know the deal behind why David did what he did," Dinero said.

We pulled into the driveway of our home. I hopped out the car before it even came to a complete stop. I wanted to hold my daughter in my arms. This was the second time that I had been away from her like this, and it hurt me to my core. I ran up the steps to my house and barged in the door. My mother and father were sitting there with

Dinelle along with Denise and Lanez. I scooped my daughter up in my arms and squeezed her so tight.

"Hey, mama," Dinelle said. Hearing her little voice tears instantly started to fall down my face.

"It's ok you don't notice anyone else," Denise said.

"Girl hush," I said, walking over to hug her.

My father walked over and kissed me on the forehead. "Hey baby girl, welcome home," he said.

"Hey, daddy," I said.

I hugged my mom and took a seat on the couch. Everyone was looking at me like they were scared to say anything. "I'm ok you guys," I lied. I wasn't ok period, but I had to be strong for my family now, especially my daughter. But, I was still gone find my son if it was the last thing I did.

My mama walked over to me "I made you guys some dishes and put them in the freezer. All you got to do is pop them in the oven and y'all will have dinner," she said.

"Thanks, mom," I said.

Dinero, Turk, and Lanez were all standing in the kitchen at the island talking amongst themselves. I knew they had something up they sleeve. I was getting tired, so I grabbed Dinelle by the hand and headed upstairs.

"Bath, mommy?" Dinelle said. I looked back at her, she be two in a few months, and her vocabulary was growing, and it amazed me.

"Yes, mommy is going to run you a bath so that you can get ready for bed. Mommy is tired," I said.

"Baby," Dinelle said, pointing to my stomach. I swallowed the lump in my throat.

"We will see baby real soon," I said. I turned the water on making sure it was not too cold or hot and ran her bath water. I added a few drops of bubble bath and used my hand to stir it in the water. I removed Dinelle's clothes and placed her in the water. I started washing her up, and I just found myself staring at her. She was cracking up playing with the bubbles in the water. I felt a single tear roll down my cheek. I wiped my face.

"Mama cry," Dinelle said.

"You want me to finish up?" I heard Dinero's voice coming from behind me.

"It's ok; I got it thanks," I said. I finished washing up Dinelle and rinsed her off. I grabbed a towel.

"Come on; step out the tub, sweetie," I told her.

She did as she was told and we walked to her room. When we got in her room, I grabbed a pull up and slid it on her.

"Sophia pajamas," Dinelle said.

I laughed and grabbed her Sophia pajamas out of the drawer and placed it over her head. “Ok, hop in bed,” I said. Dinelle did as she was told.

“Night night, mama. Lub you,” she said.

“I love you too, goodnight,” I said. I turned on her night light and cut the light out to her room.

Walking into our bedroom, Dinero was sitting up in bed watching old episodes of *The Wire* he was addicted to that show. I hopped in the bed and snuggled up under his arms, taking in his scent. “You smell good,” I said. He chuckled

“That’s what a shower does,” he said.

“You tryna say I stink?” I asked, sitting up looking at him.

“I mean, you said it,” he said.

“Shut up fool,” I said, thumping him.

I hopped up and headed in the bathroom to start a shower. When I walked in, the Jacuzzi tub we had in the bathroom was filled with bubbles and rose petals. I turned around.

“You’re too much. What if I hadn’t come in here?” I asked. Dinero hopped out the bed walking over to me.

“Oh, your ass was gone get in this tub, one way or another,” he said. “Just go in there and relax, don’t fall asleep on a nigga either,” he said.

I removed my clothes and placed my body in the tub. Dinero walked back in the bathroom.

"Baby, why did you keep this phone?" he asked, holding up the phone Ms. Gabby gave me. I shrugged, "That phone is the little piece of hope I have in finding our son," I said leaving it at that. Dinero nodded, leaving me alone with my thoughts.

I finished up and removed my body from the tub. I grabbed a towel and wrapped it around my body. Dinero had me a pair of boxers and one of his t-shirts laying out. He knew I love to sleep in his things. I smiled and put the clothes on. Once dressed, I climbed in bed with Dinero. I laid on his chest and used my finger to draw circles on his six-pack.

"Girl, you better be lucky you just had our son," he said, smacking me on my ass. I busted out laughing.

"Well, my mouth still works," I said as I reached down into his boxers and pulled his dick out.

My mouth watered instantly at the chocolate snake looking at me. I placed my body in between Dinero legs, facing him and giving him direct eye contact. I spread his legs wide, which caused him to jump

"Oh, hold up what are you doing? A nigga ain't feeling this with my legs spread open like a bitch," he said. I shook my head.

"Just trust me, do you trust me, Dinero?" I asked. He sighed

“Don’t touch my ass, Kyra.” He said. I nodded. I wasn’t about to touch his ass no way. I placed one hand around his shaft and then took my tongue and glided it up and down. I stopped then use my hands to hold open his legs and placed my mouth completely over his dick covering it. Making sure it hit my tonsils. I knew he loved my head because a bitch had no gag reflex. I continue to move my mouth up and down over his dick while holding his legs open. I removed my mouth and looked at him.

“Look at me,” I said. Dinero looked at me, and I grinned.

I spit on his dick and used my hand to jerk him off. I placed my mouth back on him still holding eye contact with him.

“Girl, you know what the fuck you doing,” he said. I felt his shit start to throb while I continued to suck him off not letting up.

“I’m coming,” he said.

“Come for me, daddy,” I said. He released in my mouth, and I swallowed his seeds.

Chapter 18

Nitro

I stood in the kitchen warming up Jr. bottle. He was hollering at the top of his lungs. “Come on son, chill out for daddy,” I said trying to rock Jr. while I waited on the bottle. This parenting shit wasn’t easy at all. Mama walked into the kitchen.

“Give me that child,” she said, reaching for him. He instantly got silent.

“The fuck,” I said.

“It’s a woman’s touch, plus he misses his mama. Look how he’s turning his head towards my breasts. He thinks I got some milk in there,” mama said. “Ain’t no milk in there, baby,” she said, laughing at Jr.

I watched as she continued to rock him side to side. I grabbed the bottle and checked the temp of the milk. It was fine.

“Give him here so I can feed him,” I said, grabbing my son. I walked over to the living room in the condo I was renting and sat down on the sofa.

I looked at Jr. ears and tips of his fingers. “Mama, was I a dark baby?” I asked.

“Nope, you came out looking Mexican. Even for your daddy to be as black as he was, you only got dark as a summer tan.”

Mama walked over to Jr and me. She looked at Jr. "Son, are you sure this your baby?" she asked. I scrunched up my face.

"How can you ask me something like that?" I asked.

"This child is gone get dark. That boy Kyra dates ain't he dark?" Gabby asked.

"Fuck him; this is my son," I said. Now shit had me thinking, was this really my damn baby.

Kyra

Lying in bed staring at the ceiling. I couldn't bring myself to sit in this house all day. I looked over at Dinero's side of the bed. He had woken up early to take Dinelle to daycare. I opened the drawer on the nightstand and pulled out the phone Ms. Gabby gave me. I powered on the phone the only contact in the phone was the number that Ms. Gabby had put in there for me to call. I press call. "Hola?" I sat up in the bed

"Um, yes, Gabby please," I said.

"Gabriel doesn't live here, but I can relay a message," the man said. "Could you please tell her that Kyra called and she can call me back on this number. I will keep it on at all times," I said.

"Ok, will do," he said.

"Thank you," I said and ended the call. I sat there in awe because I was one step closer to finding my son hopefully.

After that phone call, I was somewhat in a good mood. I hopped up and headed towards the closet and looked for me something to put on. I pulled out a pair of Saint Laurent high-rise metallic gold jeans and a Saint Laurent sequined top. Yeah, that would look real nice. I turned to my shoe side and grabbed a pair of Christian Louboutin floral velvet boots. I carried the clothes back into my room and laid them across the bed. I grabbed my towel and hopped in the shower.

When I got out the shower, I stood in the mirror looking at my little stretch marks. My stomach was still trying to go down. I walked over to my dresser and grabbed a small girdle to hold my stomach in. I slid into the pants with ease. Dinero walked into the room.

"What are you getting all dressed up for?" he asked. I was putting my shirt on.

"This is not dressed up baby. I can't step into my place of business where I sell fashion looking crazy," I said.

"Wait, why are you going to the shop? I already have someone taking care of things for you until you ready to go back to work. Why you can't just chill? You just had a baby, Ky," he said.

"Dinero, I'm not about to sit in this house and go crazy not doing shit all day. I have to keep my mind busy before I fucking go crazy. And you don't have to remind me that I just fucking had a baby. I know what I pushed out of my pussy!" I yelled. Dinero held his hands up

"Whoa, ok I'm gone need you to calm down. I didn't mean no harm in nothing I said, baby. I understand we both have our different ways of dealing with this. How about we go to the shop, and you get acquainted with the staff and stuff. Then we go to lunch?" he asked, grabbing ahold of my hands.

"I guess, Dinero," I said. I removed my hands from his and walked back in the bathroom. "Ugh these eyebrows need handling," I said.

I applied some hair lotion to my curls and played around with my hair until my curls were how I wanted them. "You gone have to take me to see my girl Jennifer so I can get these eyebrows handled," I told Dinero.

"That's cool, baby," he said.

Dinero

I was somewhat shocked at Kyra snapping off on a nigga. I knew she was hurting. It wasn't like a nigga was trying to intentionally keep bringing up the fact about her having a baby to try to hurt or anything. It was just I wanted her to take it easy and let me handle things for her. That shop was gone be there. She has yet to tell me everything she endured while with Nitro. I wonder if they slept together during that time. Knowing Nitro, I wouldn't put it past him.

"I'm ready," Kyra said, snapping me out of my thoughts.

She was looking beautiful as always. When she walked past me, I grabbed her hair. I loved Kyra's hair. She had the biggest head full of curls. Dinelle had the same shit like her mama.

"Boy, stop pulling on my damn hair," she said, smacking me in the chest. We walked out and hopped in my Bentley. "Go to Jennifer's first, I ain't going nowhere with these eyebrows looking like this," Kyra said.

"Man, hope they asses don't be taking all day," I said.

Pulling out of the driveway, I turned the radio on we bobbed our head to Moneybagg Yo's "Trending".

"I walk in a room full of bosses and you know I'm blending, she say I'm a hood nigga with no sense but bitch I got plenty," I rapped with Moneybagg Yo.

We hit the interstate and headed towards Nashville. I hated this drive from Brentwood back to the hood. I watched Kyra pull her burner phone out her purse, and she sighed and put it back in her purse. *What was that all about?* I asked myself.

"Why you keep checking that phone?" I asked Kyra.

"Nothing, I just don't want to let it go, it's the only thing I have that may help me find our son. Speaking of which, when he comes home he doesn't have a name," Kyra said, looking at me.

"I haven't really thought about that," I told Kyra being honest. She looked back out the window, and then she turned back to me

"Kyro, that way he will have both of our names," Kyra said.

I nodded "Whatever you want, baby," I said. I pulled into Jennifer's and parked.

"I'll be back," Kyra said, getting out the car.

Jennifer's was in the middle of the hood; it had a little bit of everything in this retail place. You could get your hair cut at the barbershop, ladies get they nails and eyebrows done at Jennifer's, and if you got hungry, you could choose from Prince's Hot Chicken or the Chinese spot down the walk. It also had a clothing store for men, a place to do your taxes, and get your windows tinted on your car at the same time.

I was sitting watching the many people come out of Prince's Chicken. They had the best hot chicken in the Ville; people would come from all over the United States to eat they chicken. I looked up and noticed Ivy coming out of Prince's. *What the fuck!* I rolled the window down.

"Ivy!" I yelled. She turned around and looked. Once she noticed it was me, the expression on her face changed. She tried to turn around and keep walking.

"Bitch," I mumbled to myself, hopping out of the car. Hitting the locks on my car, I ran up to her and grabbed her arm.

"Why the fuck you running? Because of that foul ass shit you pulled sending that shit to my girl." I asked. She rolled her eyes.

“I never sent anything to your girl; that was Nitro’s doing. I just recorded it and sent it to him,” she said.

I looked at her up and down; something was off, I just couldn’t put my finger on it.

“Nitro is a fucking fungus that just can’t be killed,” I said. “I’m sorry if I caused any problems. I can do my part and apologize. I kind of needed to talk to you anyways. You hard to find these days,” she said.

“A lot of shit been going on, but what’s up?” I asked.

“I’m pregnant, Dinero,” Ivy said. I felt like all the life had been sucked out of me.

“Girl, go head on with that shit,” I said. I turned to walk back to my car.

“Dinero, I have no reason to lie to you,” she said still walking behind me.

“Ivy, you're a whole stripper out here, ain’t no telling how many niggas you done let run up in you raw,” I said.

“I don’t care what the fuck I do for a living. I don’t fuck niggas at my job and definitely, don’t let any and everybody run up in me raw. This is your baby, Dinero!” she yelled.

“Bitch, say what?” I heard Kyra’s voice coming from behind me.

"Shit," I said, running my hand down my face. Kyra came around to where Ivy and I stood.

"What the fuck did you just say?" she asked Ivy. Ivy leaned to the side.

"I just told your man here that he has a baby on the way," Ivy said. Kyra turned to look at me. "So not only did you cheat on me with this bitch, but you fucked this bitch with no motherfucking condom?" Kyra yelled. I could tell she was pissed.

"Look, we can handle this shit another time; it's freezing out here," I said.

"It ain't shit to handle. Wrap this shit up so you can take me home," Kyra said, walking off and getting in the car.

I turned to Ivy who was standing there with this look of happiness on her face. "A nigga ain't no deadbeat, so if that's my child, I'll be there. But whatever crazy ass things you got going through your head like if you think we gone be together or some shit, you might as well cancel that shit like Nino," I said. I grabbed her phone and put my number in her phone. I opened the door and hopped in the car and dipped.

Kyra wasn't saying shit and honest to God that shit was scaring me. Kyra had been through too much shit, and she wasn't the same person. So, her silence was killing me.

Kyra

Can you imagine the pain I feel right now? I wasn't expecting to come outside and hear the things I heard. This bitch was carrying his child. Really and this nigga has yet to say anything. I'm leaving. Yep, I'm not about to deal with this shit. I could forgive the cheating but a whole damn kid, hell fucking no. My leg was shaking vigorously I just wanted to hop in the driver seat and whoop his ass.

"Kyra, please say something," he had the nerve to say. "Do you want me to get Dinelle?" he asked. I turned to look at him.

POP!

I hit Dinero with a right hook. He grabbed his face shocked at the fact that I had punched him. "You lucky that's all I got for you right now since you're driving," I said.

Dinero pulled up at the house, and I hopped out. I hurried up the steps into the house. I headed straight towards the bedroom closet and started grabbing me some clothes and putting them in a suitcase. Dinero came in.

"So, we not gone talk about this Kyra, you just gone leave a nigga?" he asked. "You gone throw all this away because of one single mistake?"

"Fuck you, Dinero. You had the chance to make those choices, and you did just that. You not having a condom should've been reason enough to not even fuck that bitch. I don't want to hear shit about you being drunk. Your black ass didn't even pull the fuck out. This is all your fault!" I yelled at him.

"Kyra, a nigga messed up one time. I haven't even seen or messed around with Ivy since then yet along someone else. You the one I want to be," Dinero said. "Baby, I'll make it up to you." I rolled my eyes.

"You always think money solves everything don't you. Well, money isn't gone fix this," I said still removing shit from the closet.

"Kyra, we need to stick together so we can find our son," Dinero said. I grabbed a stiletto and threw it at the back of his head.

"No, the fuck you will not use my baby in this shit. I will find my own child while you deal with the new one you got on the way," I said. I grabbed the suitcase and headed downstairs. I grabbed the keys to one of Dinero's many rides. I walked in the garage and hit the locks on his Mercedes G-Class. I threw my luggage into the back.

"How the hell you gone leave but take my shit?" Dinero asked.

"Easy, just like this," I said starting the car up and pulling out of the garage.

"Kyra!" he yelled.

I kept driving having no clue where I was going. I drove to the nearest gas station and called Di'mond, Kyng's wife.

"Hey, girl," Di'mond answered.

“Hey Di’mond, I’m sorry to call you, but I sort of need your help,” I said.

“What is it?” she asked.

“Dinero and I got into it, and I left, and I was wondering if I could stay at your condo since it’s just sitting there, just for a little while?” I asked.

“Girl, sure meet me there,” Di’mond said.

“Thank you,” I said.

“No problem. See you in a few,” she said, and we disconnected the call.

Chapter 19

Dinero

Everything was beyond fucked up now. Kyra's ass done left and Ivy ass is fucking pregnant. I took a sip of the Hennessy I was drowning my in sorrows, and with the other hand, I held a bag of ice on my eye because Kyra had hit a nigga good. My phone beeped, and I instantly grabbed the phone hoping it was Kyra calling. I didn't recognize the number, so I hit ignore and laid the phone in my lap. About two seconds later another beep came through, and it was a text from the number that I ignored.

It's me, Ivy, the text read.

I sighed and called Ivy back. "What man? You done caused enough damage for one day," I said.

"Dinero, I'm sorry I don't want you to think that I'm some messy ass person that's just tryna come in your life and start some shit. Hell, if I hadn't seen you today I probably would've went on and not even told you about the baby," she said.

I instantly thought of Kyra and how she kept her pregnancy with Dinelle a secret from me.

"Look, shit ain't gone be easy, but it is what it is," I said.

"I just want to co-parent for our child," she said.

"If, it's my child that's all it will be," I said, clarifying that. "Dinero I swear to you this is your kid, I was with nobody else unprotected at the time. Anyways I have a sonogram in the next two weeks to see the sex of the baby. Do you want to go?" Ivy asked me.

"Yeah, just let me know the details closer to the date," I said.

"Ok. Talk to you later," Ivy said.

"Aite," I said, ending the call. I took another sip of the Hennessy. I wanted to call Kyra, so I dialed her number. The phone rang once and went straight to voicemail. She really hit a nigga with the ignore the button.

She thinks a nigga can't find her, but I keep tracking devices on all my shit since she took a nigga ride.

Kyra

I had met Di'mond at her condo in Downtown Nashville. I grabbed the suitcases out the car and carried them to the elevator. I stepped into the elevator and pressed 12. My phone beeped, and I glanced down and saw it was Dinero calling. I pressed ignore and threw the phone back in my purse. The elevator came to a stop, and I stepped out the elevator heading to apartment 1215. I knocked on the door. The door flew open, and Di'mond pulled me in for a hug.

"Oh, girl come here," she said.

I dropped the suitcases I had and hugged her. I liked Di'mond. Even though she and her husband were literally made of money, she remained down to earth and not some snobbish ass bitch. I walked into the apartment that would be home for me for a little while.

"What is going on girl?" Di'mond asked, taking a seat in the living room.

"Girl, what isn't going on. From being kidnapped and held hostage for four months, giving birth to a child that was just snatched away from me and only God knows where he is at. To me thinking that things between Dinero and me would finally be good, only to find out the stripper bitch that he cheated on me with is now carrying his child. I don't think I can take anything else happening to me," I said, spilling everything to Di'mond.

Di'mond stood over and walked to the stocked bar and poured me a glass of wine.

"Here." She said handing me the glass. "So where do you see you and Dinero now? Are you ready to just end it all? Don't give these bitches what they want, especially the chick that is carrying his baby." Di'mond said.

"It's just so hard to overlook that shit. We got a whole kid out here that is missing. I haven't even got to experience being a happy family with him since we got together. Every time we take steps forward something pulls us back. This shit is getting old. I just really need a break right now," I said.

"Well, I'm not telling you to forget what he did, but if you see he ain't worried about that chick and just wants to be a father to his child, then let him. We don't do deadbeats around here," Di'mond said. I nodded my head and finished off my glass of wine.

"Hey, I know you have people in high areas. I really need help trying to find Nitro and my son," I said.

"Do you have any leads?" Di'mond asked. "The only thing I have is this Nurse Gabby that delivered Kyro and helped me. I called the number that she had put in the phone and left a message for her to call me," I said.

"And they found you in Bowling Green, right?" Di'mond asked.

"Yes," I said.

"Ok give me some time, and I'll see what I can do. In the meantime, you get some rest wake up and conquer the world. Try even talking to your man. You can stay here as long as you like," Di'mond said.

"Thank you, girl, you are such a blessing," I said.

"No problem," she said.

I walked over to the window and took in the amazing view of Nashville at night with all the lights. It was beautiful. I grabbed my phone and called my mother.

"Hey, ma. I was just calling to let you know I'm about to come get Dinelle," I said.

"What is going on now, Kyra? Dinero came by here looking for you," she said. I rolled my eyes.

"We will talk when I get there," I said. Hanging up the phone and calling Dinero. I didn't want to talk to him right now, but I wanted to know what he had to say since he been blowing up my phone.

"Kyra," he said, I could tell he had been drinking.

"What is it Dinero, what you want?" I asked.

"Where are you?" he asked.

"It doesn't matter, I'm somewhere safe," I said.

"Come on Ky, please don't do this to us. I'm so fucking sorry. If I could take it all back, I promise you I would. A nigga fucked up big time, I know that now. I can't go on without you though. I need you by my side to see me through this bullshit. I already told Ivy what it was and how things were going be," he said. I rolled my eyes.

"So, you talking to this bitch already and I ain't been going two damn hours," I said. I'm sorry y'all I was pissed.

"Look, for one Kyra I'm not about to be no deadbeat to my kid," he said.

"You don't even know if the kid is yours yet, Dinero," I said.

"It doesn't matter, Kyra. I would feel fucked up if I'm not there for her then the baby gets here and it's mine. That means I still neglected the mother of my child. I wouldn't do that to you, and I'm not about to do it to Ivy. Now when the child gets here and it's not mine that's a whole other story. But, I know I messed up and fucked her without a condom, and the timing is right, so it's a huge possibility that I'm the father," Dinero said.

"Are you done?" I asked. I was not about to sit here and continue to listen to this shit.

"Really Kyra?" Dinero said.

"Yes, really. No matter how you try to fix this up and spin it. I still feel the same. I'm not asking you to be a deadbeat to a child. I have a right to be angry, hurt, and mad. So just because you are over the shit, doesn't mean I'm gone get over it that fast. Like yeah, it's ok it's just one kid. I need space. Kyra is tired of fucking hurting. I shouldn't have to sit and look at another bitch enjoy her pregnancy when I can't even enjoy being a mother to our other kid. So, like I said, I need time to get through this!" I cried out and slammed the phone down.

Denise

"I swear I don't know why folks don't believe in answering phones these days," I huffed as I climbed the steps to my brother's house. I pulled out my key and inserted into the lock. The house was completely dark.

"I hope they asses ain't up here fucking," I said, climbing the steps. I walked passed Dinero's office.

"Denise, what are you doing here?" Dinero called out when he saw me walk pass the door. I turned around and went into the office. I flicked the lights on.

"What the hell are you doing sitting in the dark and where's Kyra? I've been calling the both of you," I said. I noticed Dinero's eye on swole.

"What happened to your eye?" I said, laughing.

"Damn Denise, this is not the time to be playing. Kyra punched me in my shit," Dinero said. I couldn't stop laughing.

"She got your ass good. What did you do Dinero? I thought y'all was on good terms," I said. Dinero rubbed his head.

"Ivy's pregnant," he mumbled. I stepped around the desk, so I could hear correctly. "What did you say?" I asked.

"Man, Ivy's pregnant. She's four months," Dinero said. I popped him in the back of his head

"How could you be so stupid? Nigga, you didn't strap up?" I asked. I threw my hands up. "I swear you niggas be doing the dumbest shit these days. I know my girl is hurting," I said, shaking my head.

That's all I could think about was how Kyra felt at this moment. "So, Kyra left yo ass, didn't she?" I asked.

"She ain't trying to hear shit a nigga saying, talking bout she needs some space," Dinero said.

"What you expect, bruh? This girl done been through hell and high water, so now you just want her to chuck it up and welcome your baby with a woman you cheated with. This shit wasn't even supposed to happen with y'all," I said. "Ain't Ivy a stripper, so you believe that this your baby?" I asked.

Dinero laid his head back against the chair he was sitting in. "Why is everybody trying to make a nigga turn on his seed?" he asked. I placed my hands on my hip and cocked my head to the side as if I heard him correctly.

"Dinero Jackson, I refuse to believe that you are being this damn stupid. Ain't nobody trying to make you do shit because it's clear you make the decisions in your life that up until this point has fucked you over. Do you really put all your trust in a woman who set you up for the next nigga? Hello, do you remember this bitch taped y'all fucking? That right there says a lot about the type of woman you just got pregnant." I yelled.

"Man, I ain't trying to hear this shit right now," Dinero said.

"Fine, because I'm done talking to your stupid ass anyway," I said, walking out his office.

"Worry about that nigga you laying up with!" Dinero yelled.

"Fuck you!" I yelled back, walking down the steps and leaving the house.

Kyra

Sitting at the kitchen table having dinner with my mom and dad was refreshing. It felt somewhat good to be home. Dinelle was sitting in her high chair tearing up her food.

"Kyra, so are you going to tell me what's going on?" my mother asked. I sighed.

"Y'all, I just wonder if I'm ever gone get to the point of being truly happy. I mean it's constantly stuff going on in my life. Dinero has a kid on the way with the girl he cheated on me with," I said. My dad started coughing, and my mom gave him a side eye.

"Daddy, I know about you too. Maybe that's what I need to do shoot Dinero so he can see I'm not playing with his ass," I said serious as a heart attack.

"Kyra, that's not the answer," my mother said, laughing.

"Well, it worked for me, all it took was one bullet, straighten me right up," daddy said. I couldn't do nothing but laugh.

"I'm serious, what am I supposed to do?" I asked.

"Baby, we can't give you the answer to that. Only you know what your heart wants. It's nothing wrong with demanding your respect. But, don't go shooting at nobody to get it. Don't let these hoes come for your spot," mama said, taking a bite of her macaroni.

"Mama, you got all this undercover ratchet in you," I said, laughing.

"I'm just saying you can have your space to get your mind right but let these hoes know you ain't went nor are you going anywhere. That is unless you just want to move on without Dinero. But, I know Dinero loves the ground you walk on, and he made a mistake. Don't stay away too long," mama said. I looked at my daddy.

"That's why I married your mama," he said.

"Oh, shut up fool, you ain't have a choice," she said, and we all busted out laughing.

Chapter 20

Dinero

It was time for Ivy to find out what she was having. It had been two weeks, and Kyra still wasn't home. We talked occasionally and communicated about Dinelle, but that was pretty much it. I found out she was staying at my homie Kyng's wife condo in downtown. That somewhat put a nigga at ease because I knew she was safe. I was on my way to scoop up Ivy and take her to her doctor appointment when my phone rang. I hit the Bluetooth on the car speaker.

"Hello."

"Dinero where you at?" Kyra's voice came through the speakers. Damn, did I want to tell her where I was headed to or not?

"I'm about to head to Ivy's doctor appointment. Is everything good?" I asked scared of her reply.

"Never mind, I'll see if Denise can do it," she said.

"What is it, Ky?" I asked.

"Nothing, go head pick up your baby mama," she said and disconnected the call. I shook my head. Lord give me the strength to deal with this shit.

I pulled up at Ivy's apartments, blowing the horn. She stuck her head out the door before coming all the way out. I watched her strut to the car. Ivy wasn't bad on the eyes and her being pregnant brought her beauty. I unlocked the door as she climbed in.

"Hey," she said when she got in the car.

"What's up," I said.

"Thank you for coming with me today. I hope I didn't interfere with any plans," she said.

"You good, where's the doctor's office at you going to?" I asked.

"It's off 23rd right beside Centennial Women's Hospital," she said. I nodded my head and pulled off.

"How's Kyra doing?" Ivy caught me off guard asking that.

"Kyra's good, working and being a good wife," I said.

"Oh, so she over the fact of us having a kid together?" she asked.

"Look, I don't mean no harm, but my relationship and my girl is not up for discussion. Matter of fact please don't even speak on Kyra. We are strictly only communicating because of the child you're carrying. Don't get shit confused," I said.

"Well excuse me I didn't mean anything by it. just trying to make conversation," she said.

"Well, make conversation about anything but my personal life," I said.

We pulled up to valet and made our way into the building. I took a seat in the waiting are while Ivy went and checked in. I watched her walk back over to me with a smile on her face.

"So, what do you want a boy or girl?" she asked.

"Shit, I already got one of each, so it really doesn't matter," I said.

I pulled my phone out and scrolled through Facebook to kill time. A nigga rarely posted anything. I just used it to see what everybody else had going on.

"Davis!" the nurse called, and Ivy tapped my arm signaling for me to come on. I stuffed my phone in my pocket and followed them to the back.

"So, you guys excited to see what the sex of the baby is?" the nurse asked. Ivy spoke up.

"Yes, this is my first child, so I'm really excited," she said. I sat down in the seat beside the bed while the nurse prepared Ivy. She turned the light off and started the sonogram.

About ten minutes into the sonogram "I think I see what the sex is," the nurse said. She typed some shit on the computer "This one has its legs wide open," the nurse said. "This would be a boy," she said.

I smiled not really realizing that's what I had done, and I grabbed Ivy's hand. She looked at me with slight confusion, and she just smiled back. I don't know something about seeing my son made me feel good. The nurse printed out some copies of the pictures and gave us both a pair. I helped Ivy sit up.

"OMG, I'm so excited. A little boy; he's gone be everything," Ivy said, typing away on her phone and taking pics of the sonograms.

"Come on, let's get out of here," I said.

Kyra

"Hang that one up over there," I told Denise.

I had been reorganizing my shop for the past two weeks getting things the way I wanted them to be. We were still open for business, and the money was good.

"Bitch, you gone have to put me on the payroll," Denise complained.

"Nah, don't even act like that because I stayed helping your ass at your shit. I don't want to plan another party ever," I said.

I walked over behind the register and checked my phone. I clicked on Facebook, and my eyes grew big. "No, this nigga didn't," I said. Denise walked over

"What?" she asked.

I handed her my phone. Denise put her hand over her mouth He didn't post this on his page, that messy ass bitch did, and she tagged him in it.

"Kyra, before you go off, calm down," Denise said.

"Calm down; now this means everybody gone know our fucking business, then she puts "*Our Jr.*" Bitch this ain't his first son!" I yelled.

I closed out of the Facebook app and dialed Dinero number. I tapped my foot while the phone rang.

"What's up, baby?" he asked. Well, Congratufuckinlations on your son but damn you gone make him a Jr.?" I asked.

"Kyra, can we talk about this when I get home, I'm dropping her off right now," he said.

"Fuck all that, when did you become this person who allows everybody to be in they business?" I asked.

"What are you talking about?" he asked.

"How do you think I found out y'all was having a boy? It's all on Facebook, my boy," I said.

"You posted that shit on Facebook, Ivy?" he asked Ivy.

"I didn't see nothing wrong with it, you were acting all happy at the doctor office holding my hand and stuff," I heard Ivy say.

"Man, I swear you hardheaded. Delete my name off that shit," I heard him say. "I'm not deleting shit, you the father of my child and you and your bitch gone have to deal with it," Ivy said.

"Bitch, I got your bitch. Fuck all this back and forth you wait to I see your ass. Pregnant or not bitch you gone get whooped into this family!" I yelled. I hung up the phone.

Denise stood there with her arms crossed looking at me. "Child, I don't know what to say about y'all. This shit is getting worse by the minute," she said. I looked up and saw Di'mond walking in carrying a manila envelope.

"Hey girl," I said.

"Hey boo," she said, kissing me on the cheek.

"What brings you by?" I asked. Di'mond handed me the envelope.

"This is a start; I got my guys still looking into it further. But I had them pull up some info about your kidnapping when it made the news. They were able to get the address of the house you were in and the name of the renter at the time was a Gabriel Sanchez. Didn't you say the nurse that helped you name was Gabby?" Di'mond asked. I felt tears start to roll down my face.

"Yes, that must be her. Did they get any information on her?"

Well, this Gabby lady was born in Mexico, and she moved to the United States. It says she has a son Nathanial Jordan. And..."

"Wait, Nathanial Jordan, that's Nitro," I said.

"This whole time this was her son. If I can find her I know I can find my baby," I said.

"Well, the trail stops there but like I said I'm going to have my guys to dig deeper see if we can get some location marks somewhere. I know she hasn't vanished off the face of the earth," Di'mond said. I hugged Di'mond.

"Girl, thank you," I said.

"I will do anything I can to help you, and you know that," Di'mond said.

Nitro

"Mama, can I trust you to stay with Jr. while I go back to Nashville and take care of some business?" I asked.

"Nathanial, you need to take that girl her baby, why are you keeping this child; he's clearly not your son," my mother asked.

I did a DNA test on Jr., and it was true he indeed wasn't my child. I had gotten attached to the little nigga.

"Mama, look shit ain't that easy," I said. I'll be back first thing in the morning. Don't leave this apartment," I said. I walked over and kissed Jr. on the forehead.

I knew it was a chance I didn't even make it back to Atlanta, but that was a chance I was willing to take. I hit the highway to Nashville.

Gabby

My son was crazy as hell thinking he gone keep me locked up in this damn house. I picked up the phone and dialed my brother's number.

"Hola," my brother spoke into the phone.

"Alejandro, it's Gabby. How is everything?" I asked.

"Oh, Gabby, things could be better when are you coming home?" he asked. "I'll will be home soon hopefully helping Nathanial with something. Has anyone called there looking for me?" I asked.

"Matter of fact yes, a girl called by the name of Kyra, she said she would keep the phone on for you to call anytime," he said.

"Si," I said. I looked over at Jr. who was still peacefully sleeping. "We're gone get you home to your mama soon, sweet boy," I said.

"Ok, thank you, Alejandro. I'll talk to you soon," I said and ended the call.

I picked up the baby. "Let's walk over here to the corner store so I can get me a beer," I said to Jr., even though he didn't understand shit I was saying. I bundled the baby up and threw on my coat and headed out the door.

We walked into the store, and I headed straight to the back to grab me a six pack of Coronas. I walked up to the counter and placed the beer on the counter, smiling at older man ringing up my beer.

"$9.78," the man said. I pulled out my debit card and inserted my chip. The man gave me my receipt as he placed the beer in the bag.

"Gracias," I said and left the store. I walked back to the apartment trying to hurry and get out of this night air.

Kyra

Sitting in my office counting money from today's sale, I was overwhelmed with happiness from the news Di'mond gave me and angry from the shit going on between Dinero and me. I knew eventually I would have to face him and we put all this nonsense to the side, but right now wasn't the time because I wanted to hurt this Ivy chick. Denise stuck her head into my office.

"You about finish? Are we about to go get some drinks?" Denise asked.

"Yeah hold on, let me lock all this shit up," I said. I placed the money in a lock box and pressed in the code on the safe. I put the money in the safe and locked it up. I didn't like making bank deposits at night so it would be safe there until the morning. I turned off the computer and grabbed my coat and purse.

We headed to Medusa Lounge to enjoy some drinks and hookah. I haven't been out to enjoy any time with my girls so tonight was the night. I knew deep down in my heart that my time was coming to an end on being without my son and I owed that and so much more to Di'mond. It made me wonder what exactly was Dinero doing? Kyng and Di'mond had the same connections so why hasn't he went to Kyng for help on finding our son.

"Can we get a bottle of Hennessy?" Denise said.

"Girl, hell no. It's a fucking weekday, and I have to be up at the shop in the morning. I need something light because if my ass drinks Henn tonight, I'm liable to pop up at your brother's and kick his ass," I said. Di'mond and Denise both started laughing.

Speaking of which let me call and see if he picked up Dinelle. I stood from the table and headed to the bathroom. I dialed Dinero. After the third ring, he picked up.

"Hello." It was Ivy.

"Bitch, why are you answering my man's phone, better yet why are you still with him?" I asked.

"He ran into Knockout Wings to get the baby and me some food. These cravings are a motherfucker," Ivy said.

"Where the fuck is my child?" I asked.

"Oh, she's in the backseat sleeping. I wonder if our son will look like his sister; she is beautiful," Ivy taunted.

"Bitch, I put it on everything I love, when I see you I'm going in your shit. I'ma teach your ass some manners!" I snapped and hung up the phone.

I walked out of the bathroom and walked back over to the table I grabbed the bottle of Hennessy out of the bucket and poured it into an empty glass. I threw the brown liquor back as it burned just a little bit as it went down my throat.

“I take it the phone call didn’t go so good?” Denise asked.

“Why did Ivy just answer Dinero’s phone, and tell me why my child is around this trick,” I said, clapping my hands while I was talking. Denise and Di’mond just shook they heads as I poured me another drink.

Chapter 21

Dinero

I walked back to the car carrying the food I got for Ivy. Dinelle was in the back knocked out, so I asked Ivy would she sit in the car with her. I got in the car and handed the bag to Ivy.

"Thank you," she said. "Oh, your baby mama called too, she was hella pissed," she said all nonchalant. I looked at her.

"I know you didn't answer my phone, Ivy?" I asked.

"I didn't think nothing of it," she said, biting into one of chicken wings. I knocked the chicken wing straight out of her hand.

"You know what, I'm peeping this game you playing. You like to start a lot of shit and then try to act all innocent. Let me tell you something. One thing you don't know about me is how I get down, and you most definitely don't know how my girl rocks. I'm warning you, Ivy, you better chill the fuck out before your child grows up without his mammy," I said through clenched teeth. This bitch had worked my last nerve. "Now pick that shit up off my floor," I demanded.

The rest of the ride back to Ivy's was silent. I didn't have shit to say to her, and I didn't care if she had shit she had to say. I know to keep this bitch at a distance. I pulled up to her apartment and waited until she got out. I didn't even wait and see if she made it in the house before I peeled out burning rubber. I called Kyra's phone, and she didn't answer. I headed home and got Dinelle ready for bed.

Ivy

I couldn't believe he snapped on me like that. Ok yeah, I did some fucked up shit, but damn. I placed the food on the kitchen table and headed to my room to undress. I put on my robe and walked back to the kitchen. There was a loud ass knock at the door.

"Who the hell is it?" I yelled, snatching the door open.

"Nigga, is you crazy, what the hell are you doing here?" I asked, standing there looking at Nitro. He made his way in the house. I closed the door making sure no one saw him walk in. He sat down on the couch and looked at me

"Who the hell done knocked you up, Ivy?" he asked. I rolled my eyes.

"None of your business," I said. "What are you doing here anyway. Speaking of which, you owe me some money," I said.

"I came back to handle some money situations, I ain't got it right now times is hard and you know I'm taking care of my son and shit," he said. My ears perked up.

"What son?" I said, playing stupid.

"I got custody of my son. My baby mama was tripping and shit, so she handed him over to a nigga," he said.

"Kyra just handed you over her child?" I asked.

"Yeah, she hated a nigga that much to where she ain't even want to raise my son," Nitro said. I shook my head *trifling bitch*, I thought.

"Where are you staying now?" I asked.

"Atlanta, with my ma. You should come visit a nigga sometimes. I do miss that pussy, you sure that baby ain't mines?" he asked.

"Boy no," I said. I wasn't about to tell him who my baby father was either. I couldn't wait to tell Dinero this shit maybe it will put me back on his good side.

Kyra

I jumped up and heard snoring. "What the fuck?" I said, turning around to see Dinero sound asleep behind me.

I saw I was dressed in a t-shirt. I looked on the floor for my clothes that I had on, and they were gone. I saw a small trash can beside the bed. I closed my eyes and thought back over my night and how the hell I got here. I remember leaving the shop and heading out to drink with Denise and Di'mond. *Why the hell did I drink so much?* I asked myself. Dinero must've felt my movement because he woke up looking at me.

"You feel better?" he asked.

"I feel like I'm supposed to be mad at you about something, but why in the hell am I in the bed with you?" I asked.

"Come on Kyra, please don't start all that. This bed is where you're supposed to be anyways. But, Denise said you got drunk as hell last night and passed out," Dinero said.

I placed my head in my hands. I felt Dinero hand rubbing my back.

"I miss us, Ky," he said.

I closed my eyes, and I wanted to jump in his arms so bad, but things just weren't right with us at the moment. Dinero sat up in the bed.

"Kyra, listen. I'm coming to you as a man, and a nigga sorry for every ounce of pain I have caused you. I realized some shit today, and I also realized that I don't want to lose you as my woman. I want to marry you one day. I feel like a nigga ain't been doing my part as your man or protector. Real talk, a nigga is fucked up without my son and it's crazy every time a nigga gets a little lead it don't be shit. All a nigga sees is us all together and happy— you, Dinelle, Kyro, and me," he said. I smiled at the mentioning of Kyro's name.

"I've been doing my own searching and I actually got some information about the nurse Gabby. Come to find out her name is Gabby Sanchez and Nitro is her son. Di'mond's got her people still working on it," I told Dinero.

"Why you ain't tell me this sooner?" he asked.

"Um, I tried, but your baby mama answered the phone. That bitch is gone make me hurt her," I said. Dinero let out a huge sigh.

"Ok, about that. We got to come to a mutual understanding and a lined of respect for each other. I understand you don't like her and it's some beef, but for the sake of my kids and our future together, I don't want no drama in my life. I'm gone talk to her to because I don't even see why she's trying to start shit because I made it perfectly clear more than once that we were co-parenting and that was it. My personal life and all that other shit was off limits," Dinero said. I looked around the room for my purse.

"Where is my purse?" I asked Dinero.

"Laying over there on the couch," he said. I hopped out of bed and grabbed my purse off the couch looking in my purse for the burner phone I carried.

"Oh no," I said.

"What Dinero?" Dinero asked.

"My phone, the one I carried for Gabby to call me on, it's gone," I said, feeling like my heart just crushed into a million pieces.

"Maybe it fell out in one of the girl's cars or something."

"This can't be happening," I said. I dropped to the floor on my knees. "That was the only way I had to get in touch with Gabby," I cried. Dinero came and wrapped his arms around me.

"It's ok we gone find him. I promise you," Dinero said.

Dinero

Kyra being in my arms felt so right. Hopefully, we could get things back on track like they should be. My phone started ringing "Let me get that," I told Kyra, lifting her up and grabbing my phone off the nightstand. I saw it was Turk calling.

"What up?" I said into the phone.

"Word on the street is this nigga Nitro showed his face in town last night," Turk said. I balled my fist up.

"You kidding me, right?" I said.

"Nah, you know I wouldn't even play with you like that. You need to check into your baby moms though," Turk said, causing my brows to furrow.

"Who Kyra?" I said, looking over at Kyra who was looking back at me with confusion on her face.

"Nah, that other chick, Ivy or some shit," Turk said. I nodded my head.

"Aw ok," I said.

"Good looking out, bruh," I said.

"No problem keep me posted on movement," Turk said.

"Bet," I said. I hung up the phone and looked at Kyra.

"What?" she asked.

"Turk said Nitro came back last night," I said. Kyra eyes got so big.

"Is that nigga still here?" she asked. I shook my head.

"Nah, I need to go over to Ivy's and holler at her for a minute," I said.

"What the hell for?" Kyra asked.

"I don't know. Nitro was supposed to have been spotted with her," I said, grabbing me some gray sweatpants to put on.

"Oh no the hell you don't, take them shits off. I wish you would step foot over there with them shits on. Might of fact, I'm going over there with you," Kyra said, heading to the closet and slipping on some leggings and her UGG boots.

"Kyra, you going over to this girl's house is not a good idea," I said.

"This is concerning my son, I'm not going over there on no foul shit, but if the bitch jumps stupid, I'm gone beat her all in her face. Her face ain't pregnant," Kyra said. I shook my head at Kyra.

I stepped into the bathroom with her and grabbed my toothbrush to brush my teeth. I watched as Kyra pulled all her hair up into a bun. I laughed. This girl thought she was slick. We headed downstairs.

"I didn't know Denise was here," Kyra said.

“Yeah, all y’all asses was drunk, I told her ass go in the guestroom, but I guess she couldn’t make it past the couch,” I said. “Come on before she wakes up,” I said, pulling Kyra out of the house.

I hit the lock on the door, and we headed to Ivy’s. The whole drive over there I had plenty of thoughts going through my head. I most definitely wondered why the hell would Nitro come back and visit Ivy. Did she know something this whole damn time about my son? I don’t know, but today we were about to get to the bottom of this. We arrived at Ivy’s. I turned the car off. I didn’t call before I came because that nigga could still be in here. I reached into my waistband and grabbed my pistol, taking the safety off. I looked over at Kyra and didn’t have to tell her shit because she was doing the same. That shit was sexy as hell how she handled a gun. She looked like the type to fear pistols. You wouldn’t look at her and know she done caught a body and didn’t mind catching another one.

“Kyra when we get in here can you please allow me to do the talking. You get a little hot-headed too quick, and I need to get as much information out of Ivy as possible. Can you do that for me, baby?” I asked. Kyra rolled her eyes.

“Yeah,” she said.

We hopped out the car, and I walked up to Ivy’s apartment. I knocked on the door. Kyra stood on the side of me, Ivy opened the door wearing a bra and some underwear, and her belly was showing.

“Um, can you put some clothes on,” I said.

“What is she doing here?” Ivy asked.

“Girl, go put some clothes on. See from here on out I see I’m gone have to be around when you come over here if she’s answering the door wearing that,” Kyra said. I looked at Kyra like hush.

Ivy came back in the living room wearing a robe. “What brings you two by?” Ivy asked.

“Was Nitro here last night?” I came straight out and asked her. Ivy looked at me with sad eyes. She was taking too long to answer.

“I told you she couldn't be trusted,” Kyra said. I looked at her like please shut up.

“You can’t fix your mouth to say shit about me, who has a baby and give it away because you don’t like the daddy,” Ivy said.

Kyra stood up and punched Ivy in her shit so hard she flew back on the couch losing her balance. “I don’t know what type a bitch you think I am, but I’m a mother before anything. You let Nitro fill your head up with stupid ass lies. You should know how that nigga operates. That man kidnapped me and kept me hostage until I had my baby, and he raped me damn near every night. I haven’t seen my child since I had him. And, the baby isn’t even his, it’s Dinero’s. Where the fuck is Nitro?” Kyra yelled at Ivy. I looked at Ivy, and she sat there looking like Kyra knocked some sense in her ass.

“I don’t know exactly where but he said he been staying in Atlanta with his mama,” Ivy said.

“That’s all he said?” Kyra asked.

“He told me I should come and visit him sometime,” Ivy said.

“Why the fuck would he tell you that, you were fucking that nigga too?” I asked Ivy not realizing I shouldn’t have asked that in front of Kyra. Kyra looked at me.

“Excuse you?” Kyra said.

“Go head on Kyra,” I said not even trying to start no argument.

“You need to stay away from that nigga,” I said to Ivy.

“How the fuck you gone tell her who to stay away from, she is not your concern. That baby is. We may need to use her ass as bait to get Kyro back,” Kyra said. I scratched my head because she did have a point.

Chapter 22

Kyra

It was now February, and I sat at my desk surfing the net researching everything I could that would possibly help me find Gabby. I had put my all into finding my son. Dinero ass should've left and headed to Atlanta the day Ivy told him that's where Nitro was. The door to my office opened, I looked up staring at Dinero. I shut the top on my computer.

"What's up?" I asked. He walked in and came around the desk to wrap his arms around me.

"I got something special planned for you for Valentine's Day." He said. I let out a huge sigh.

"Baby, I appreciate it but Valentine's Day is the last thing on my mind right now," I said.

"I know baby, but you need to take a break, you been drowning yourself in nothing but work and this Gabby lady. I'm not saying stop what you're doing, but at least let me give you more than what you deserve," Dinero said.

"Why does it feel like I'm the only one concerned about finding our son?" I asked, getting up and walking away from him. Dinero looked shocked, but this was just how I felt and had been feeling from some time now.

“Really Kyra, is that how you feel? Just because I don’t jump when you say jump I don’t care about my son?” Dinero said.

“Exactly, that’s your son out there. You have the means to get an army of niggas out there to look for our child, but you are sitting back working like a snail planning irrelevant ass shit that I can give two shits about right now!” I yelled.

“I can’t believe you are saying this right now. It’s a way to move when dealing with certain folks. We already know this nigga don’t give a shit about nothing but that baby, but he wouldn’t hesitate to kill you or me to protect what he thinks is his. I got a million-dollar bounty on this nigga head. I don’t run everything by you, Kyra. But, don’t fix your mouth to tell me I don’t care about my flesh and blood!” Dinero yelled back. “I know what this is really about. You're upset because I didn’t send Ivy down there,” Dinero said. I placed my hands on my hip

“You right, I am,” I told him. Dinero shook his head.

“You know, despite how you feel about Ivy that is still the mother of my child. What I look like sending her down there putting her and my child in harm’s way. I’m not that type a nigga. If this nigga knew she was carrying my child, he would hurt her and my kid. Nitro will do anything he can to fuck with me. So, you right, sorry for being a man about the situation. I be glad when Kyro does come home because this Kyra right here, I’m not feeling,” Dinero said, walking out of my office.

"Fuck him," I said.

Dinero

Kyra was tripping. I understand her pain, but to point fingers and accuse a nigga about not giving a fuck about his child was an all-time low for her. They say everybody has a way of showing emotions, but she's steady pushing a nigga away. I sat in the parking lot of the shop just thinking about what just went down. I opened the glove box and pulled out the Tiffany box that had the two-carat engagement ring in it. The sound of my phone snapped me out of thoughts.

"What up, Kyng?" I said in the phone.

"How did everything go?" he asked me. I closed the ring box.

"Man, Kyra's on some other shit right now. Bruh, I seriously think if I don't find Kyro soon, it's a wrap between us. She feels a nigga just sitting back not doing shit. I mentioned Valentine's Day and she went off on a nigga. You know any other time a female ain't about to be calling Valentine's Day an irrelevant ass day," I said.

"Oh, damn. She's just going through it right now that's all. Don't hold anything against her. She will come around soon enough," Kyng said.

"Yeah, I sure hope so," I said. My line clicked, and I saw that it was Ivy.

"Bruh let me get this, it's Ivy," I said.

"Aite," he said. I clicked over.

"Yeah," I said.

"Dinero, something is wrong. I think my water broke, but it's way too early for this!" she yelled in the phone.

"Did you call your doctor? Is this normal?" I asked.

"I don't know, and she told me to get to the hospital right away. I'm heading there now," Ivy said.

"Aite, I'm on my way," I said, hanging up the phone.

I was about to back out the parking lot when I glanced up, and Kyra was standing at the door looking out the window at me. I should've told her about Ivy, but what the hell did she care. I continued backing out and headed to the hospital. I arrived at Women's Centennial Hospital in ten minutes flat. I walked in the hospital and headed to the Labor and Delivery floor.

"Ivyanna Davis?" I asked the nurse at the nurse's station.

"Second door on your right, down that hall," the nurse replied. I turned and headed towards the room. Walking into the room Ivy was hooked up to all these monitors, and I could tell she had been crying.

"What's going on?" I asked her.

"They said my water did break which is something called Preterm Rupture. My water broke, but I'm not in labor. Some shit I don't know it's too much," Ivy said.

“Excuse me, can you tell me what’s going?” I asked one of the nurses.

“Well, since she is twenty-six weeks, we need to keep this baby in her as long as possible and hope infection doesn’t set in. Her water did break, but she isn’t in labor. We are going to monitor her very closely and get her started on steroids. If at any time we feel the need to deliver, we will. But, she is to remain here in the hospital on bedrest until she delivers. That’s the safest thing for her and the baby,” the nurse told me.

“Ok, thank you.” Now that I had a better understanding of what was going on, I walked over to Ivy.

“Everything is gone be ok, so don’t trip out or nothing,” I said.

“I can’t have him right now, I don’t want my baby to die,” Ivy said. I grabbed Ivy’s hand.

“Look, stop thinking negative. Everything’s gone be straight.” I told her.

I stepped out into the hall and called Kyra. She didn’t answer so I left a voicemail. “Um, Kyra I was calling to let you know that Ivy’s water broke and we’re here at the hospital. She hasn’t gone into labor, but they are monitoring her closely due to her being so early. I was just letting you know. Love you, Ky,” I said and ended the call.

Kyra

I listened to Dinero's voicemail that he left me telling me what was going on with Ivy. I could hear the concern in his voice. I know a bitch be tripping and stay wilding out on Ivy, but I don't wish no harm on her baby. I know she's probably losing her cool right now. I had made it home and was fixing a batch of Shrimp Alfredo for dinner. I had Pandora playing on the refrigerator. I was in love with my Samsung refrigerator. I stirred the sauce on the stove and took a sip from my wine glass. The doorbell rang, and I placed my glass on the counter to answer the door. I looked through the glass and saw Di'mond smiling. I opened the door and let my girl in. Di'mond was beautiful; she favored Cassie.

"Girl, what you are doing over here?" I asked. Di'mond stood in a Wonder Woman pose.

"Who do you love and why?" she asked. I looked at her like she was crazy.

"What you done did now?" I asked.

"Check this out. I got three hits on Gabby using her debit card in Georgia. Two hits came from Lithonia and one from Conyers." Di'mond showed me the locations on the paper. "I suspect they may be staying in Lithonia because of the use at this convenience store." Di'mond said. I nodded my head.

"Bitch, I swear you the shit," I said.

“Girl, you forgot who my daddy was. If that nigga can fake his death for years and still move about freely, he can find somebody if he needed to,” she said. I walked back to the kitchen to check on my sauce.

“You want a glass of wine?” I asked Di’mond.

“That’s not even a question,” Di’mond said, grabbing her a glass out of the cabinet and pouring her some wine.

“I’m going to Atlanta Di’mond, even if I have to go by myself,” I said. I had never been more serious in my life. “I’m bringing my son home,” I said.

“You not gone tell Dinero?” Di’mond asked. I leaned on the counter.

“Dinero has some other issues that he’s dealing with right about now. Ivy went into labor,” I said. Di’mond lifted her brow.

“Oh, wow I thought she wasn’t due to the beginning of June?” Di’mond asked. I nodded my head.

“Yeah, she is so I can only imagine what she’s going through. I know I don’t too much care for her ass, but I don’t wish no harm on that baby,” I said. “Tomorrow, I’m dropping Dinelle off at my mom’s, and I’m going to Georgia. This is between you and me, not for you tell your man or Denise’s nosey ass,” I said.

“I’m not saying shit. What you gone do while you’re there?” Di’mond asked.

"I'm gone rent me a car and hotel and just start casing places, starting with them locations you gave me. I need to get ahold of some guns because I can't be driving down no highway carrying weapons and shit then my ass be locked up." I laughed.

"I got some people in Atlanta. I can hit them up and tell them to be expecting you. They will fuck with you and if you need some back up they with the shit also. Let me get you Maceo's number," Di'mond said, grabbing her phone and scrolling through the contacts. She placed the phone on speaker.

"What it do, Di'mond?" Maceo voice came through the speakers sounding like God.

"Hey, yella ass boy. How you been?" she asked.

"Mane, shit been cool. You know me staying low and on the go," he said.

I ain't gone lie whoever this nigga was she was on the phone with voice was so deep and smooth I felt my panties melting off right there. I took another sip of the wine.

"Look, my home girl is coming to Atlanta, and she needs some assistance with some things, so I need you to look out for her and help her. Her name is Kyra, and I'm gone give her your number so she can give you a call," Di'mond said.

"Ok, fo sho. I got shawty. You know I fucks with you," Maceo said.

“Thanks, hun, I owe you,” Di’mond said, pressing end.

Di’mond looked at me, and I was standing there fanning myself. “Kyra, stay the fuck away from Maceo like that. You got enough shit going on in your life,” Di’mond said, cracking up.

“Girl, what. I can’t help it. He sounded good as hell on the phone,” I said. Di’mond shook her head.

“Give me your phone so that I can put his number in there,” she said. I handed her my phone and let her put Maceo number in. I was heading to Atlanta, and nobody was stopping me.

Chapter 23

I barely slept a lick last night because I was so anxious to hit the road. I laid there looking at Dinero empty side of the bed. I rubbed my hand over his spot where he would normally lay. I wanted to call him and make sure everything was ok. I grabbed my phone off the charger and dialed his number. His phone went straight to voicemail. I rolled my eyes and dialed the number again, and the same thing happened. After the beep, I left a message.

"Hey, it's me. I noticed you didn't come home last and I was just calling to see if everything was ok with you and the baby. I may not be here when you get home, but I will call you soon enough. Love you," I said and sent the message.

I laid the phone back on the dresser and threw the covers back getting out of the bed. I slid my feet in my house shoes and went to the bathroom to take care of my hygiene.

After getting my hygiene together and getting dressed for my trip, I headed to Dinelle's room to get her up.

"Fat mama, wake up," I said, rubbing her face. She opened her eyes and immediately started smiling. "Good morning," I said helping her out of bed.

"Me hungry, mama," Dinelle said.

"Ok, I'll fix you something when we get you dressed for granny and papa's ok," I said.

We headed into her bathroom and removed her pull up and washed her up and brushed her teeth. I walked into her closet and grabbed her a jogger set to put on. After she got dressed, I rubbed some SheaMoisture milk in her head and pulled her curls into a ponytail.

"Come on, let's go fix you some cereal," I said, walking downstairs.

"Daddy," Dinelle said.

"He's not here, you will see him later," I told Dinelle, fixing her a bowl of Cheerios and slicing her up some fruit.

While Dinelle was eating her breakfast, I sat at the table scrolling through Facebook. I noticed a post that Ivy had posted and tagged Dinero in. *Please keep our son Dinero Jr. in your prayers, he was born last night 14 weeks early so far, he is being a fighter, but things are critically for him right now.*

"Damn," I said. I called Dinero the phone just rang and then eventually went to voicemail. *Why isn't he answering my calls*? I looked over at Dinelle

"You finished?" I asked. She nodded her head yes. I cleaned up her mess and grabbed our things to head to my parents' home.

I pulled up at my parents and grabbed Dinelle and her things out of the car. I used my key to let myself in the house.

“Mama, Daddy!” I yelled. My mom came around the corner wiping her hands off on her apron

“Kyra, why is you coming in here keeping up all that fuss?” mom asked.

“I’m sorry,” I said, placing Dinelle bag on the couch.

“Um, what’s that for?” mama asked. I smiled.

“I need a favor. I have to go out of town for a while, and I need someone to keep Dinelle. Her daycare is paid up so you can take her to daycare whenever you want,” I said. Mama shook her head.

“Now you know I don’t mind keeping my grandbaby, but where is her father? Is she going with you?” she asked.

“Ma, no he is not going with me plus Ivy had her baby last night, and it’s not looking too good, so I haven’t really talked to him,” I said.

“Why are you not at the hospital with your man at a time like this?” mama asked.

“If he wanted me there he would return my phone calls. The only reason I know what’s going on is because she put it on Facebook. I have to go. This is something that I can no longer wait on. When I get back you can meet your grandson,” I said.

“You found the baby?” mama asked me shocked.

“Not yet but I found the nurse, so I have a friend that’s going to help me. Please don't say anything to Dinero because I don’t need to hear his thoughts on what I’m doing. I got to go. I love y’all,” I said, leaning in planting a kiss on my mom's cheek and bending down to kiss Dinelle. Atlanta here I come!

Dinero

I stood on the other side of the glass watching the nurses and doctors stick all these tubes in my son and put him in an incubator. I had never seen something so fucked up in my life. They were working fast because it was critical that my son get the best medical attention. I was paying top dollar for care for my son. My phone had been dead for hours, and honestly, I’m glad it was because I didn’t want to talk to anybody. I headed back to the room to check on Ivy. I walked in the room, and she was glued to her phone.

“They getting it together for him, how you feel?” I asked her. “I’m fine. It’s nothing else I can do it’s in God’s hands now,” she said. I nodded my head in agreement and sat down in the chair beside the bed.

“Jr. is a fighter; I know he is,” Ivy said.

Ivy named him after me by making him a Jr. I didn’t put up no fight because at the time seeing him like that and not knowing if he was gone make it or not. It just felt right.

“I’m gone head home and get cleaned up, put on some clean clothes. I’ll be back up here later,” I told Ivy.

“Ok,” she said. I grabbed my coat and things and walked out of the room.

Walking out of the hospital, the sun was shining a little different. I hit the lock on my car and hopped in. I sat in the car and let it warm up for about ten minutes before I pulled off. I placed my phone on the charger so that I could get some juice. If I know Kyra, I know she blew my phone up especially since a nigga didn’t come home last night. I sighed because I really didn’t have the energy to go back and forth with her right now.

When I got home, I noticed Kyra’s car wasn’t there. I parked the car and made my way up the steps in the house. The house was clean and quiet like no one had been there. I went to our bedroom and saw the bed still messed up from this morning. I plugged my phone up and powered it on. Taking off the clothes that I had on, I threw them in the pile that I carried to the cleaners and my underclothes in the dirty clothes basket. When I walked in the closet, I saw a few empty hangers on Kyra side and some of her clothes had been thrown around. *The fuck is all this shit on the floor?* I said to myself. I walked out and headed to the bathroom to take a shower.

The whole time I was in the shower I was wondering where the hell was Kyra at? I was expecting her to be home and ready to go off on a nigga. I hopped out the shower, grabbing a towel and wrapping around my waist. I went and grabbed my phone off the charger. I had plenty of missed calls, voicemails, and texts. I played my voicemails, and I had one from Kyra. It made me smile because she was calling to check on nigga and the baby. Maybe she was coming around after all. What stood out was what did she mean about not being here when I got home. Maybe she had some things to take care of today. I dialed Kyra's phone and waited for her to answer.

"Hello?" she said her voice was music to my ears.

"Hey baby, I got your voicemail. My phone was dead plus everything that was going on, I just kept it off," I said.

"How is the baby?" Kyra asked, catching me off guard.

"It's still critical with him and seeing him with all them tubes in him fucked a nigga up," I said.

"Well, I'm praying everything be ok with him," Kyra said.

"Where you at? I want to see you before I go back to the hospital." I told Kyra. I heard her sigh, "I had to leave town for a little bit, Dinelle is with my mom," she said.

"What the fuck you mean you had to leave town? Kyra, I know you ain't heading to Atlanta?" I asked.

"Dinero…" she started talking but my line beeped, and it was Ivy.

"Ky, hold on. This is Ivy; it may be something about the baby," I said. I clicked over, and Ivy was screaming in the phone.

"Dinero, they saying they gone have to life flight him to Vanderbilt! It's not looking too good, and he needs to be with specialists!" she said, crying in the phone.

"Ivy, I'm on my way. Are they taking him now? Do I need to come there or go straight to Vanderbilt?" I asked.

"Go to Vanderbilt because nobody will be there with him I'm still in this fucking hospital," she cried in the phone.

"Ok, I'm on my way," I said. I clicked back over to finish talking to Kyra. "Fuck," I said she had hung up the phone.

Kyra

I had arrived in Atlanta, I didn't know where I wanted to get a hotel at, so once I got to downtown Atlanta, I pulled up at a gas station and called Maceo. The phone rang several times before he answered.

"Who dis?" he answered the phone. My eyes rolled in the back of my head, something about his voice done something to me.

"Hey, this is Kyra. Di'mond's friend. She had given me your number," I said. "Oh, what's up shawty, you done made it here yet?" he asked.

"Yeah, I just pulled up at a gas station to call you. I was about to try and find me a hotel," I said.

"What gas station you at, I can give you directions to me?" Maceo said. I looked around "I'm at the Shell station on John Wesley," I said.

"Cool, I know exactly where you at. I stay about twenty minutes away on Mount Paran Road. I can give you the address, or I can have someone come to you. Whatever you want to do, shawty," he said. I smiled at his accent.

"Can you text it to me and I will put it in the GPS," I said.

"Cool, I'll see you in a few," Maceo said.

Shortly after ending our call, a text came through I put his address in the GPS and was on my way to meet this Maceo guy. Atlanta was pretty, and the traffic reminded of how Nashville's traffic was now. I rented a Chevy Camaro, nothing fancy for the drive down here. About twenty-five minutes later, I pulled up to a gated home. It was beautiful; a little bigger than my house.

"Hmm he got a little taste," I said. I rolled the window down and pressed the intercom on the gate.

"That you shawty?" he asked.

"Yes, daddy," I wanted to say but didn't. "Yes, it's me," I said.

The gate opened, and I drove in. I drove up the long driveway and parked in the front. I know I looked a mess from that drive down here. I didn't have on shit fancy but a pair of Seven7 jeans and a Giorgio Armani sweater and a pair of Prada booties. I fluffed my hair up before exiting out of my vehicle.

I walked up to the door and was greeted by the finest man. I was praying this was Maceo. He stood about 6'3. He wasn't skinny, but he wasn't huge. He was just right. I could tell he worked out because his arms were toned. He had a goatee that was dirty blond, and he wore shoulder-length dreads that were the same color and to top it off this nigga had a set of gray eyes. I felt my mouth getting dry, and that was probably because I had that bitch wide opened. I heard him laugh

"I know you cold. You can come in and look as long as you want," he said. I blushed from embarrassment and stepped in the house

"I am so sorry," I said, trying to apologize.

"It's ok; you're easy on the eyes yourself. Di'mond hangs with nothing but bad bitches and she always has," he said. "You got bags or anything? I know you ain't come all the way here with no luggage," he said.

"Oh, it's in the car, I was gone find me a hotel, so it was no point in getting them out the car," I said.

"Girl, give me your keys. This big ass house and you think I'm about to have you staying in a hotel. Di'mond told me to look after you. Plus depending on how I need to assist you in some things. I don't need you to far away from me," Maceo said, grabbing my keys out of my hands.

I watched him walk to the car. This man's gone be every bit of trouble, and I know it. He walked in carrying my bags. I closed the door behind him and locked it.

"Thank you," I said.

“Come on I’ll show you where you’re sleeping,” he said.

I followed him upstairs and down a long ass hallway. He made a right into a room. I walked in, and the room was beautiful. It reminded me of a damn Versace catalog. I laughed

“Look, don’t be laughing at my room, a nigga ain’t got no female to help decorate shit, so it’s Versace everything,” he said. We both fell out laughing.

“It’s ok; I actually like it,” I said.

“Well, I’ll let you get settled. Whenever you’re ready to catch me up on things, I’ll be in the entertainment room. Just go up the other set of stairs, and you will see it,” he said.

“Ok, thank you, Maceo,” I said.

I watched him close the door behind him, and I fell back on the bed. I kicked off my boots and stared at the ceilings. *Remain focused Ky, you here to find your son and get the fuck back to Nashville,* I told myself.

Chapter 24

Dinero

I had been sitting at Vanderbilt in the waiting room for what felt like hours, I know it was hours because when they told me Jr. passed I couldn't move. I was devastated. I held his tiny body in the palm of my hand. Ivy wasn't doing too good; they had transported her here to say her goodbyes to him as well. This shit was terrible. I felt a hand grip my shoulder I turned around to see Kyng standing there.

"Oh, hey man," I said. Kyng walked around and took a seat beside me.

"Sorry for your loss, man," he said.

"Thanks," I said. "Shit kind of feels fucked up when one minute you're looking at your child then the next they gone. I swear now I know exactly how Kyra felt about Kyro," I said.

"Where's Kyra at anyways?" Kyng asked me. I shrugged my shoulders.

"I don't even know. I came home and she was gone. And when I spoke to her, she got to talking about she had to leave for a while, but she'll be back. I told her ass she bet not be in Atlanta, but I know Kyra's hardheaded, and I bet that's where she at," I said.

"I'm sure Di'mond know where she's at, but Di'mond she's hard to break. If she knows anything she ain't gone say shit. I can try and ask her though," Kyng said.

"Man, I gotta go up here and check on Ivy, then I'm gone stop by your crib before I head home," I said.

"Aite, bruh," Kyng said. We dapped each other and parted ways.

I walked up to the room where Ivy was sitting.

"I'm ready to go home. I'm sick of these fucking hospitals. No need for me to stay, it ain't like I got a kid anymore," Ivy said.

"You can do whatever you want to do, I'm sure they will discharge you," I said. "I'll go talk to the doctor and see what I can do," I told her.

Within thirty minutes Ivy was being discharged from the hospital. When we got in the car, it was complete silence. I looked over at her, and she just stared blankly out of the window.

"You hungry?" I asked. She shook her head no. We continued to drive in silence to her house. She finally spoke.

"I guess you and Kyra can go back to being a happy family. I'm sure she would love to hear that Jr. died," Ivy said. I looked at her and my eyebrow lifted.

"Ivy, if you must know Kyra was actually praying for him, y'all may have had issues, but Kyra didn't want nothing to happen to our kid," I said. Ivy laughed.

"I bet she did pray for Jr. She prayed for him to die," Ivy said. I shook my head.

"Look, I know your upset and hurt but don't try to bring Kyra into this," I said. Ivy sat up and looked at me.

"Really Dinero? Our son just died, and you're taking up for your bitch," Ivy cried. By now, I was getting pissed.

"What I'm trying to figure out is why are you even bringing her up. I just lost my child too, and Kyra knows what it feels like to lose a child, so you really need to chill, ma. Things happen for a reason, and only God knows why he took our little man. I'm sorry, and I know you angry but taking it out on other people is not the answer," I said.

I pulled up at her house, and she grabbed her things to get out the car. I was gone offer to help her in the house, but she had me fucked up.

"Can you please let me know of memorial arrangements for Jr.?" I said. She slammed my car door. I shook my head.

I drove to Kyng's crib before heading home. I had to talk to Di'mond and hoped that she knew where Kyra was at. When I pulled up to Kyng's, he and Di'mond were getting out of the car. I pulled up behind them and got out.

“Hey, Dinero. I’m sorry to hear about your son,” Di’mond said, hugging me.

“Thanks,” I said. Kyng opened the door, and we entered the house. I stood in the foyer.

“I really didn’t plan on staying long. I just came to see if you knew anything about Kyra and where she might be?” I said, facing Di’mond.

“I know me and Kyra share a lot of things, but she didn’t tell me where she was going. I think she knew y’all would know to ask me,” Di’mond said. Kyng looked at Di’mond.

“Di’mond, don’t be playing with this man if you know where she at. He got too much shit going on, and he needs to get in touch with Kyra,” Kyng said with authority.

“I just know she in Atlanta, and that’s it.” Di’mond walked off with a major attitude.

“Thanks, man, after I handle these arrangements with Ivy for Jr. I’m heading to Atlanta,” I told Kyng.

“I’m right behind ya; I got some folks down there that wouldn’t mind helping,” Kyng said. I nodded and gave Kyng dap and heading home.

Kyra

I woke up realizing that I had dozed off when I laid across the bed. *Damn*, I thought. I slid my feet into a pair of slides I had in my suitcase and followed the directions Maceo had given me to the entertainment room. I peeped my head into the door checking to see if he was in there.

"I thought you was like fuck a nigga," Maceo said, scaring me. "I saw you coming. I got cameras in that hall," he said. I smiled and eased myself into the room, taking a seat in one of the plush leather chairs.

"I'm sorry, I guess when I laid across that bed, I didn't realize how tired I was. I needed that tho," I said.

"No need to apologize, I wasn't tripping," he said. He muted the TV and looked at me.

"So, what's up tell me about Kyra," he said, catching me off guard

"What do you want to know?" I asked.

"Everything, but I'll settle for whatever you tell me," he said.

"Well, let's see. When I was nineteen I got pregnant by my current boyfriend, but end up going to jail for a year and six months because I took a charge for my boyfriend at the time who I thought cared about me. When I came home my current boyfriend and the guy I took the charge for where in business together. A lot of cheating was going on within our circle. I became pregnant again by the guy I took a charge for, and we had broken up, and I got with my current boyfriend. they fell out something terrible, and shit started getting hectic. I was kidnapped at five months pregnant by the guy who I was pregnant by. He held me hostage until I gave birth.

When I had my son, I instantly knew that it was my current boyfriend's child. The guy kidnapped my baby and left me for dead. So that brings me here to Atlanta because I have reason to believe he is here, plus the nurse that delivered my baby is his mother. I have picked up some locations here in Georgia where she has used her card. Oh, and I murdered a man and am not to be fucked with because I'm cold in the gun department and my sniper skills are A1," I said all in one breathe. Maceo looked at me in awe.

"Damn, I felt like I just read one of them fucking urban books. Girl, what haven't you been through?" Maceo asked. I shook my head.

"I've been through a lot, and I just want to live a peaceful drama free life, but it seems like no matter what, shit just follows me," I said.

"What's this nigga name that got your son?" Maceo asked me.

"Nitro is his street name, but his real name is Nathanial Jordan," I said.

"You got any pictures of that nigga and what's his mama name?" Maceo asked.

I pulled out my phone and went to my photos finding a picture of Nitro. I sent the picture to Maceo's phone.

"His mama name is Gabriel Sanchez. She goes by Gabby and, Di'mond said she might be in the Lithonia area," I told Maceo.

He nodded his head and was typing away on his phone for a good five minutes.

"I got my people on it, but tomorrow we gone go to that store in Lithonia and talk to the person running that bitch," Maceo said. I nodded my head.

"Thank you," I said.

"No problem, beautiful," he said, causing me to blush. "Now I know it's a little late, but that's when shit get popping in the A, so how about I take you out and show you how we get down," Maceo said.

"Shit, I'm down. How I need to dress?" I asked him. Maceo licked his lips.

"Make it sexy," he said.

I ran to the room to dig in my suitcase for something. A girl always came prepared. I kept it real simple by throwing on a Fashion Nova Rebecca Strip jumpsuit and topped it off with a pair of Balenciaga over the knee boots. I put on a pair of earrings and some lip gloss and was ready. I stepped out, and Maceo was coming out of the bedroom across the hall. He looked up.

"See, that's what I like a chick that don't have to put all that makeup shit on. Girl, you so damn fine," he said. I laughed.

"Um, you are aware that I have a man," I said, having to remind myself because the thoughts I was having about Maceo was not good at all.

"Yeah, you got a man, but shit, I can't help but to like what I see. I'm human. What happens in Atlanta stays in Atlanta," he said.

"I thought that was for Vegas," I said.

"Yeah, there too. Let's go, girl," he said, taking my arm in his and leading me downstairs.

Maceo and I walked into Compound Atlanta. I swear just off how everyone was acting, I knew Maceo had to be that nigga in Atlanta. Not that I wasn't used to this because Dinero had shit on lock back home. I guess anybody who had any kind of ties to the St. Clair Cartel was doing good.

"You good?" Maceo asked me.

"Yeah, I'm straight," I said, bopping to the music.

Maceo passed me a glass of champagne I shook my head no and pointed to his cup.

"Oh, you want what the big dog drinking," he said, handing me his cup. I smelled it, and it smelled like Patron. I threw the cup back and continued dancing.

After about two hours my ass was bent.

"Maceo, can we go? I'm not feeling too good," I asked. He laughed and wrapped his hands around my waist

"See, I tried to give you a girly drink, but you wanted to keep throwing my shit back like it was water," he said.

His warm breath hitting the side of my neck was doing something to me. I turned around and planted my lips on his kissing this man like my life depended on it in the club. I felt his hands go down and grab my ass.

"Let's go!" he said, grabbing my hands and pulling me out the club.

I don't even remember the drive back to his house. All I know is I woke up with Maceo's face between my legs. I looked down at this man feasting on me as if I was the last supper. I closed my eyes and felt him stick his tongue in my pussy. He was sucking on my insides while I grinded on his fingers. He lifted his face, and his goatee was covered in my juices.

"Girl, you need to be called Georgia Peach cause you are so juicy," he said.

Maceo reached over in his nightstand and grabbed a condom. He ripped the package open with his teeth, and I watched him roll the condom over his fat, long dick. *Jesus this man was about to rip me a new hole,* I thought. He spread my legs a little wider and used the tip of his dick to tease me by rubbing it up and down my pussy lips. I felt myself getting hot. "Stop teasing me!" I moaned out.

“You ready for this dick?” he asked.

“Yes,” I said, pulling him towards me.

He slowly entered me. I tensed up a little, but he eased inside. After he got comfortable and the pain had subsided, he started putting in work. I was matching his thrusts. He flipped me over.

“Get on top of this dick,” he said as he laid flat on his back watching me climb on top of him.

I placed my hands on his chest and bounced up and down on that dick, next thang you know I was creaming on that dick, Bobby Brown Tenderoni on that dick, I was about to claim that dick, grab a pen, and write my name on that dick. I picked my pace up, and he grabbed my waist.

“I’m bout to cum,” I told Maceo.

He lifted me up and place me on all fours as he entered me from the back. I was clenching my pussy muscles on his dick, and after about three more pumps we both came together. Maceo pulled out and headed to the bathroom to remove and flush the condom. I stood and walked into the bathroom with him.

“I see why these niggas are going crazy over your ass; you got that good shit,” Maceo said.

“Oh, so you about to get crazy on me?” I asked.

"Nah boo, I want to be that peace you need in your life. I'm not asking to be your man because it's obvious you got one. But a nigga is here, ya feel me?" Maceo said.

I took in what he said.

After washing up, I was heading back to my room for the night. I need to sleep all this shit off.

Chapter 25

Dinero

A couple of days had passed, and Ivy and I were still butting heads. She didn't want to have a memorial for Jr., and I wanted to. She was really getting on my nerves.

"Look, I was trying to stay around and do this with you for Jr., but I have some things I need to take care, so I'm leaving town for a little bit," I told Ivy.

"You going to find your other child?" Ivy said sarcastically. I looked at this bitch like she was crazy.

"See, this is why I can't be around you. You make a nigga want to cuss your ass out. Before you came along Ivy, I had a life. I have two other kids. The world didn't stop at you. I'm going on with my life because I still have to be a father for my other children. I can't mourn with you because you won't allow it. I have no clue why you are so angry at me because I haven't done nothing but be by your side during this. I wish you the best, and I will call and check on you from time to time, but I got to go," I said, telling Ivy and leaving her where she sat.

I called Kyng to let him know I was on the way. It was time to go to Atlanta and get both of my babies.

Kyra

Ever since that night with Maceo, things between us had blossomed. I was having fun. Being with him made me feel free and at peace. We had finally made our way to Lithonia. We were sitting outside the convenience store where Gabby's card had been used.

"You want me to go in there or do you want to do it?" Maceo asked me. I looked at the door.

"I probably have a better chance if the clerk a man," I said. Maceo phone rang, and he looked down at the screen then answered.

"What it do?" he said. I was wondering who was on the other line because all he was doing was nodding his head.

"Ok, bet. Good looking out," he said and ended the call.

"Looks like your nigga Nitro been working with some cats pushing a little minor weight here and there to stay afloat. He hasn't gotten on anybody's bad side. But my sources say he lives in Conyers, and his mom stay here in Lithonia." Maceo looked around. "In those apartments right there," Maceo said.

I looked at the apartments across the street, and all these thoughts filled my head. I was so close to my son I could feel it. *I was here; mama is here*, I thought.

“All those apartments, what am I supposed to do, go knock on all the doors?” I asked. Maceo laughed.

“I got the address that depends on how you want to do this. We can get your son, or we can make this nigga suffer. Either way, she’s gone lead us to where we need to be,” Maceo said, putting the car in drive and driving off. When we got across the street to the apartments, Maceo was creeping trying to find the apartment number.

“This is the building right here,” he said. He backed his car in a spot further away from the building. “Somebody’s got to come out that bitch sooner or later,” he said.

“I want to shoot that nigga’s head clean the fuck off,” I said.

Maceo opened a secret compartment in the car, and three guns were sitting there looking pretty. “You get to take your pick. From the way, you were talking you can shoot anything, right?” he asked.

“Hell yeah,” I said.

My phone rang, and I looked down and saw that it was Dinero. I held my hand up signaling for Maceo to be quiet.

“Hello,” I answered.

“Kyra, you still acting like a child and not gone tell me where you at?” Dinero said.

“Dinero, I told you I was taking care of something,” I said,

"Well, I'll be I Atlanta in about another hour or so," Dinero said. I changed the subject.

"How is the baby?" I asked. The phone grew silent.

"He didn't make it," Dinero said. I placed my hands up to my mouth. "Wow, I am truly sorry about that. Are you ok? How is Ivy?" I asked.

"Thanks, baby and I'm aite I watched him take his last breathes, so that's kind of sketched in a nigga head. Ivy was tripping big time we've been butting heads ever since. We didn't even have a memorial," he said. I shook my head because Ivy was a piece of work.

"I'm sorry I wasn't there to be there for you, but I had to leave. Anyways I got to go, so I will catch up with you later," I said. I laid my head on the seat and sighed.

"Is everything ok?" he asked.

"Yeah, issues at home and he's bringing his ass to Atlanta," I said. Maceo phone started ringing next. "Damn hotline," I said.

"Ooh, let me find out you jealous," he said.

"Whatever boy," I said.

"What's up?" he said into the phone putting it on speaker.

"What up nigga, this Kyng," I heard the voice say. My eyes grew big I looked at Maceo.

"Big money, what it do?" Maceo said.

"On my way to Atlanta and I need help with a problem," Kyng said. I shook my head no and was waving my hands. Maceo was looking at me like I was crazy.

"Well, just hit me when you touch down, I'm kind of tied up in an important business matter so I'll see what I can do," Maceo said.

"Aite nigga," Kyng said.

"What was that all about?" Maceo asked me.

"Kyng is with my boyfriend. I can't be around you whenever you all link up. Plus, I want this shit for myself. I want to take him out," I told him. Maceo shook his head.

"Even if I don't help him, he's gone go to the bigger dogs that helped me. So, we gone be getting the same information," Maceo said.

"Well take me back to my car, and I'll come back and finish watching the place.

"You sure?" he asked me.

"Yeah, I come back to your later. Just make sure them niggas are gone," I said. Maceo started up the car carrying me to get my car from his place.

"Thanks," I said to Maceo as I was getting out of his car.

"Make sure you keep me posted and be careful. You want me to send somebody with you?" he asked.

"Nah, I'm a big girl," I said.

I closed the door and hopped in the Camaro heading back to finish watching Gabby's place. My phone beeped, and I saw it was Di'mond calling me.

"Hello." I sang in the phone.

"Bitch, why haven't I heard from you since you been in Atlanta?" she asked me with an attitude.

"Girl, things just been moving really fast, and I've been busy. I'm so close to getting my son and knocking Nitro's ass off the map," I said. Di'mond smacked her lips.

"How has Maceo been treating you?" Di'mond asked. I smiled.

"Maceo has been a wonderful host," I said still smiling.

"Kyra Mitchell! I know you didn't?" she said.

"What are you talking about?" I asked, trying to play stupid.

"Please tell me you didn't fuck Maceo?" she asked me.

"Ok, I won't tell you," I said.

"I can't believe you." Di'mond laughed.

"Dinero's gone fuck you up Kyra. Why did you do that?" Di'mond asked me.

"It just happened, he pulled me in from the time I heard his voice," I said.

"Well, you know they on the way down there, right?" Di'mond said.

"Yeah, he just brought me back to my car. I'm about to head back over Gabby's," I said.

"Be careful, Kyra," Di'mond said.

"I will. See you when I get back," I told her.

"Ok," Di'mond said, and we hung up.

Dinero

When we got to Atlanta, we met up with this cat Maceo. I could tell he was doing good by the way he was living. We were chilling in his theatre room smoking a blunt and shooting shit about Nitro. I looked down on the floor beside the couch and noticed a pair of Pink Merino Wool Gucci slippers. Now normally I don't be peeping shit but it kind of caught me off guard because Kyra had the exact damn pair. Now, a nigga knows they didn't stop when they made her pair, but they were a very distinct pair of shoes. Instead of the normal Gucci slides everyone wore, Kyra had these for the winter. I was so caught up in the damn shoes that I had withdrawn from the conversation altogether.

I heard Maceo say, "Man, don't you hate when girls stay the night one night and they start leaving shit around like they live here," He said.

We all laughed, and I brushed the thought of Kyra out of my head.

After talking with Maceo, he was having us meet up with one of his guys that had given him some info on Nitro. From what we were told Nitro was moving a little work in Atlanta, not how we were doing it in Nashville though. He was under the radar and trying to keep a low profile. He had a little low, low spot in Conyers, and we were riding out that bitch. I wanted to talk to Kyra to let her know what was going on.

When we left Maceo's, we headed to our hotel to catch some sleep for the night because tomorrow shit was gone get real. On the drive back, I was still in deep thought about Kyra, I have no clue but something wasn't sitting right with me, and it was something about that nigga Maceo that was rubbing the wrong way.

"Aye, how well you know that nigga Maceo?" I asked Kyng. Kyng kept his eyes on the road and turned the music down just a bit.

"Maceo's a cool cat. He's been down with the family for a long ass time. That's Di'mond's cousin on her father side. Why you ask?" Kyng said. I scratched my beard and sighed.

"I don't know, but it's something about him that's speaking to me on an ill vibe. I might be tripping and overthinking, but if Kyra is down here, how is she moving, you know especially for someone who doesn't know shit or anybody down here," I said. "She just picks up and comes to Atlanta off the wam?" I said to Kyng. He nodded his head.

"Here you go with that vibe shit. What are your chakras out of line?" Kyng joked, busting out laughing.

"Nigga, I'm for real. That shit ain't funny. Then when we were at that nigga's crib I peeped them Gucci slippers, and it's just weird because I bought Kyra the same exact pair," I said.

"Bruh, you tripping. Maceo don't know no damn Kyra, and if I know anything Kyra's ass ain't fucking around on you. She ain't that type. Now if Di'mond did hook them up it was on some business type shit because that nigga's got clout her in Atlanta. But, Di'mond would've said something because she knows when I come here who I link up with," Kyng said.

I nodded my head and looked out the window. Maybe a nigga was tripping.

Kyra

It was damn near midnight, and I was getting sleepy. I reached in the backseat and grabbed me, Red Bull. I popped it opened and took a sip. My phone ringing startled me. I grabbed the phone.

"Hello," I said.

"Olivia Benson, you still out playing detective?" Maceo asked. I laughed at his joke.

"I see you got jokes, but yes," I said, watching a brand new Cadillac Escalade pull up to the building. The driver side door opened on the truck and I was staring at the motherfucking Nitro himself.

"He's here!" I yelled in the phone trying to hold my composure. My trigger finger was itching.

"Kyra, just calm down watch and see what apartment he goes to, and if he leaves, follow him," Maceo said.

"Ok, ok," I said.

I ended the call and watched Nitro walk upstairs and enter his key into the first apartment on the right. I was so nervous that I couldn't stop moving. I was shaking the hell out of my legs. I don't care how long I have to sit here, but I was not leaving this spot.

About fifteen minutes later, I saw Nitro exit the apartment carrying a car seat. Ms. Gabby came out right behind him and locked the door. They both walked downstairs and headed to the truck that Nitro had gotten out of. Nitro placed the car seat in the back seat and closed the door. I screwed my face up. *Where y'all going this damn late?* I said to myself. The truck started up and backed out of the parking spot. I laid back in my seat as Nitro drove by. When I heard the truck pass by I sat back up in my seat and started the car to follow them.

I kept my distance. I had to make it not look so obvious that he was being followed. Good thing he hopped on the interstate. I was able to stay back a great distance. We drove for what seemed like fifteen minutes. That's when I realized we were in Conyers.

"Lord, whatever you're doing thank you," I said. I continued to follow Nitro, and we pulled into some apartments, I looked at the name

"Terraces at Fieldstone," I said aloud to myself so that I could remember where to come to.

Once I saw Nitro park at the building up ahead, I pulled in immediately at the building before so he wouldn't see me. I watch Nitro and his mother get out of the truck again and Nitro grabbing the car seat. They walked into the building, and I lost sight of them. I backed out of the spot and drove towards the building driving past Nitro's truck. They were nowhere in sight, so I wrote the plate number of Nitro's truck down. I drove off smiling because I would have my son back tomorrow and everything will be ok once I kill Nitro once and for all.

Chapter 26

Kyra

The long drive back to Maceo's I cried the whole entire drive. Finally, I can see my son. I wonder what he looks like now. He was about to be a month old, and I've missed so much already. I wonder was he a crybaby, did he sleep through the night? Did he have a head full of hair like Dinelle? I cried so hard that when I pulled up in Maceo's driveway I just sat there. The fact that both of my children were taken away from me at birth was bothering me. Giving birth while in prison my child was shipped off within two days of me having her. With Kyro, I thought would be different and I would be able to enjoy the very moments I missed with Dinelle, but to have him also taken, this feeling was starting to become all too familiar. I didn't know what Dinero's plan was, but I was done having children. I wanted to give every ounce I had to Dinelle and Kyro because they deserved it and so much more. I grabbed a handkerchief out of my bag and wiped the tears that stained my face. Before I got out of the car, I texted Maceo letting him know I was at the door.

Maceo stood in the door as I made my way out the steps. He looked fine as ever with his dreads pulled up on top of his head. He had on a pair of gray sweatpants and a wife beater. I walked in and immediately his scent tickled my nose. I hugged him, and he closed the door.

"You look tired as fuck," he said. I kicked my shoes off.

“I am, plus I got a lot of stuff on my mind,” I said. I walked upstairs to the guest room I was staying in and laid across the bed.

I felt Maceo walk into the room behind me. He laid across the bed and pulled my hair out of my face.

“Talk to me, Kyra,” he demanded in a soothing tone. I looked into his gray eyes.

“You know after tomorrow when I get my son back that this right here we’re doing is a wrap,” I said. I wasn’t trying to be hurtful, but this was wrong anyways on so many levels. Here I was snapping out on Dinero for cheating and getting a bitch pregnant, and I turn around and cheat on him.

“I figured that much,” Maceo said.

“When I get back to Nashville, I don’t know how the hell things are gone pan out between Dinero and me, but I do know I want to work on my family. Dinero and I have been on a rollercoaster ride of bullshit from the jump. I think once Kyro is back home things between us will get better,” I said.

“Are you gone tell him about our little rendezvous?” Maceo asked. I shook my head.

“I don’t think I can,” I said truthfully. I rolled over on my back and looked at the ceiling. “The only thing on my mind right now is seeing the blood splatter from Nitro’s head when I shoot that bitch dead,” I said.

"What you gone do about his mama?" Maceo asked.

"Nothing, she saved my life and I know she the one been looking after my son. She just better keep her old ass out of the way because if I have to, I will shoot her ass too." I said.

"So, can a nigga get some going away pussy since you gone leave a nigga with a broken heart tomorrow?" Maceo asked. I hit him playfully.

"See, don't do that and no, we need to stop this right now," I said. Maceo laughed.

"It's cool. At least I got a taste and feel. All bullshit aside though I won't disrespect nothing you got going on, but whenever you need a nigga for whatever, just call me. I'm your friend before anything." Maceo said, kissing my forehead.

We both laid there and continued talking to we both fell asleep.

Dinero

I woke up bright and ready to handle this shit today. I've been waiting on this day for far too long, and I get to lay eyes on my son who I have never seen. After taking a shower, I threw on my get dirty gear, nothing but all black down to the shoes. I placed a black skully cap on top of my head and headed to Kyng's room.

I stood in the hallway outside of Kyng's room while he continued to get dress. I text Kyra.

GM Ky. Today is a new day and a good one at that.

Smiling, I placed my phone back in my pocket. Kyng came out the room, and we dapped each other.

"You ready to do this?" he asked.

"Nigga, ready ain't the word I said. We stepped on the elevator ready for war.

Kyra

I woke up the next morning feeling a bit off. I didn't know what it was, but my stomach contained a nervous feeling. Maybe I was just too excited about the events that were taking place today. I looked over at Maceo who was sound asleep his dreads covering his face. I got out of bed and went and got myself together for today. I went to the bathroom and sat on the toilet as I rolled me a blunt. I normally didn't smoke, but today called for a blunt. As funny as it may sound, my senses were on point and better when I smoked.

After I finished rolling my blunt, I laid it on the sink until I finished up with my hygiene. Stepping in the shower, I washed my body then I washed my hair. I wrapped a towel around my head when I finished and stepped out of the shower. Drying off and rubbing my body down in coconut oil. I felt a little bit better. I picked up the blunt and sat on the edge of the tub and took it to the head. I heard a knock on the door.

“Damn, you thought I wasn’t gone smell that gas you smoking through the door,” Maceo said. I laughed.

“You can come in!” I yelled.

Maceo opened the door and walked in the bathroom with a grin in his face. He leaned up against the sink, and I passed the blunt to him. He grabbed it from my hands and took a hit.

“Well, today is the day. A nigga glad I could help get you what you needed in finding your son,” Maceo said. I smiled and nodded my head.

“I’m forever grateful for Di’mond and you, I swear from the time I told her about my situation, she came through off top. And you have been very helpful also with your southern charm and hospitality,” I said. He passed me the blunt and I refused.

“I’m good; I need to start getting dressed and make sure I have everything packed and ready to go,” I said while exiting the bathroom.

After getting dressed, I made sure I had everything in my suitcase. I walked into the bathroom and grabbed my toiletries. Once I had everything I zipped up my luggage and carried it downstairs. I placed the luggage by the door and waited on Maceo. I pulled out my phone since I hadn’t checked it all morning. I smiled when I saw a text from Dinero. I texted back.

Good morning baby. Yes, today will be a great one. I love you too forever and always. Soon as I get home, I’m gone make it all up to you, lol.

I put the phone back in my purse and Maceo came downstairs, carrying a black box. "

You ready?" I asked him.

"Yep, but I got something for you before we go," he said, handing me the box. I shook my head.

"You don't need to do nothing else for me," I said.

"Girl, hush and open the box," he demanded.

I rolled my eyes and opened the box. When I opened the box, my mouth flew open it was a Gen4 Glock silver and Tiffany Blue with a built-in laser light. It had my initials engraved on the side.

"Boy, you done showed out," I said, holding the gun in awe.

"I knew you would like it, don't put too many bodies on that," he said. We both busted out laughing.

"Let's ride," I said.

Dinero

We pulled up to the apartments where this nigga Nitro is supposed to live. We parked in the lot across from his building. I had my gun sitting in my lap.

"How you want to do this?" Kyng asked.

"I'm gone place the call asking that nigga to come outside; he thinks he's meeting somebody to catch a sale. When that nigga come to the car, we get him in this bitch. I'll handle him, and you get the baby. I don't give a fuck who's in that house. You can kill them all for all I care," I told him. Kyng nodded.

Kyra

Maceo and I pulled up at the apartments that I came to last night. They looked way different in the daytime. It looked to be a rather quiet area. I parked where I parked last night. His truck was still parked in the same spot.

"What you want to do?" Maceo asked. I looked around, and I saw my spot.

"You see those trees over there?" I pointed to a set of trees that stood side by side each other but extremely close. "Those trees line up with his truck. I'm gone walk over to that building and take my spot between those trees. When that nigga come to the car, this pretty pistol you gave me is going go to work. As soon as he hit the ground, I'm walking straight to that apartment and grabbing my son," I said.

I grabbed the pistol and put it in my waist. The coat I had on was perfect, and it concealed me. I threw the hood over my head and exited the vehicle.

Dínero

Dialing Nitro's number, I pressed call on the phone.

"Hello." He answered on the first ring.

“Aye, yeah, this Cash, I’m sitting outside of your apartments,” I said disguising my voice.

“Aite, here I come,” He said.

“Bet,” I said, dropping the phone and picking up my pistol. Kyng grabbed his gun. We were ready.

A few seconds later Nitro exited the apartment carrying a car seat.

“Well, this nigga just made this ten times easier for us. Who the fuck brings a kid to a drug transaction. We watched as he came down the stairs.

Kyra

I stood in between the trees with my hood covering my head. I was dressed in all black like the omen. I wore a pair of black leather gloves. I looked up and saw Nitro coming out of the apartment. It was like time stood still and everything was moving in slow motion. I noticed when he started making his way downstairs he was carrying Kyro.

“Well, I don’t have to buy no car seat,” I mumbled.

Nitro walked to the car and opened the back door, placing the car seat in the backseat. When the door shut and he opened the front door, I lifted my gun aiming at his head.

BOOM!

I fell back and looked up at Nitro's truck, which had engulfed in flames. I saw Nitro's body halfway in and out the truck. The fire was so bad, and that's when it hit me.

"KYYYYYRROO!" I yelled, running across the street.

Folks had started coming outside. I looked up, and Dinero and Kyng were running over.

"What the fuck did you do?" I yelled at Dinero hitting him in his chest. "I told you I had this!" I yelled.

Trying to make my way in the truck, I was pulled back by someone trying to keep me from being burned. I ran over to Dinero and kept hitting him.

"Kyra, I ain't do that shit!" he yelled.

"Somebody, please help, my baby is in there!" I cried. The truck was burning so fast.

"Everyone needs to get back in case it explodes some more," a bystander said.

I notice Maceo walking over to where I was standing. I ran to him and started crying in his arms.

"Somebody put a bomb in that truck, and my baby was in the backseat," I cried. I felt Maceo rubbing my back consoling me as I cried.

I heard the ambulance and fire truck coming in the background. But not before I heard, "What the fuck is this shit?" Dinero barked.

I felt all the color drain from my face forgetting that I was even in Maceo's arms.

To Be Continued...

CPSIA information can be obtained
at www.ICGtesting.com
Printed in the USA
LVHW01s2320120618
580568LV00009B/275/P